G000081784

The Archimedean Heart

The Archimedean Heart

BJ Sikes

San Sarlagiin Press, 2016

Copyright © 2016 BJ Sikes
All rights reserved. This book is a work of fiction. Names, characters, businesses, organizations, places, events and incidents either are the product of the authors' imaginations or are used fictitiously. Any resemblance to actual persons, living or dead, events, or locales is entirely coincidental.

ISBN-13: 978-0-9974375-5-3
Printed in the United States of America.

Cover design by Eloise Knapp
www.ekcoverdesign.com

For Aaron

Brittle Beauty

Brittle beauty, that Nature made so frail,
Whereof the gift is small, and short the season;
Flowering to-day, to-morrow apt to fail;
Tickle treasure, abhorred of reason:
Dangerous to deal with, vain, of none avail;
Costly in keeping, past not worth two peason;
Slipper in sliding, as is an eel's tail;
Hard to obtain, once gotten, not geason:
Jewel of jeopardy, that peril doth assail;
False and untrue, enticed oft to treason;
Enemy to youth, that most may I bewail;
Ah! bitter sweet, infecting as the poison,
Thou farest as fruit that with the frost is taken;
To-day ready ripe, tomorrow all to-shaken.

—Henry Howard, Earl of Surrey

Prologue

Paris, 1870

John's mother lay dying. Her once-delicate nose jutted from her shrunken cheeks, spider-webbed with wrinkles and spotted with age. She turned her face into the shadows, seeming to be unwilling to show him the wreck that had once been a lovely face.

"Thou farest as fruit that with the frost is taken," John muttered, his throat tight. She who had been the epitome of all that was beautiful deserved poetry but the poems that came to mind were not those she would appreciate. His chest constricted with pain and he swallowed back tears.

"What did you say?" she said. "Come closer, I cannot see you." Her voice wheezed at him from the bed. He rose from his chair by the window and stood over her, unsmiling.

"I am here, Mother. You should rest."

She reached up to grasp his hand and he suppressed a shudder of disgust. Her hand felt cold and dry, the skin yellowed and hanging from the bones like a badly made bed.

"I will have an abundance of rest soon. Until then, let us talk," she said. "Help me sit up." Holding his breath to avoid inhaling the stench of age and sickness, he gently pulled her frail body into a sitting position. He arranged pillows to support her then stepped back.

"Ah, my dutiful son, always here to do exactly what is required but no more," she said. John frowned in response, his mouth tight with unspoken words.

"What more do you need, Mother?"

She shook her head and exhaled, her breath rattling in her chest.

"Pay no attention to me. I am just a babbling old woman. If only you really wanted to be here with me. I miss your father. He always wanted to be in my company. I was his everything." Her eyes grew distant. John quelled his surge of anger. She always had something to complain about; even on her deathbed, he would not be good enough. He was so tired of hearing about his saintly father, a man who died when John was young. But it was too late to hope for anything different from her. Too late for anything. She would be dead in a few days at most, the doctor had said. John closed his eyes and squeezed the bridge of his nose, struggling to control his emotions.

"John! Are you still there?" she said, her voice shrill. He moved closer to the bed.

"Yes, Mother. I am right here."

She reached out and grabbed his hand again, pulling his head down to her face. He averted his gaze from hers, hoping she wouldn't detect his abhorrence to her wasted body.

"John, you must continue to paint. You could be a great artist someday. Paint beauty. Always paint beauty. Do not indulge yourself like these modern painters and their whores. You must remain pure. Do you understand me?"

Her tone demanded his obedience and he obeyed as he always had. His face hidden from her, he grimaced, his eyebrows drawn close together.

"Yes, Mother. I understand. I will not fail you. I promise you, I will stay pure. I'll—" His words dried up, his throat closing.

She nodded, her head unsteady. She watched him with thoughtful eyes, absent-mindedly scratching a rash on her wrist.

"One more thing, then you must go and let me sleep." She let his hand go and gestured towards a thick packet of papers tied with string on her nightstand. "Take those letters."

John raised his eyebrows and picked up the packet.

"Whose letters are these?" he asked, turning them over in his hand. The paper looked old, the ink faded.

"You must introduce yourself to Henri Desjardins. Those are his letters to your father."

John's curiosity was piqued.

Henri Desjardins? The artist? Why would an artist correspond with my father? And so long ago? Surely Desjardins would have been just an adolescent when my father was still alive.

"These letters are from the artist Henri Desjardins?" John asked. The old woman lay as if asleep. "Mother?"

He reached down and nudged her shoulder. There was no response.

One

Montmartre, 1880

John sat on the patio of the *Bistro du Royales* studying the old flower seller. The sky changed color as the sun rose over the Paris rooftops and he let his eyes roam up to drink it in. The dust and smoke had been washed down by that night's scheduled rain, leaving the air fresh and clean. He smiled, relaxing in the stillness of the morning. John was alone on the patio; it was too early for any of the bistro's usual aristocratic clients. A discarded newspaper sat on the table in front of him. Catching sight of the headlines screaming of lynchings, his breath caught in his chest. He hoped that his colleague had arrived from America safely.

John sipped his *cafe au lait* and studied the flower seller anew. She sat amidst her baskets of orange and yellow chrysanthemums on the church steps opposite the bistro. Parisians passed her on the street and she turned her wizened face up to greet them. John studied the lines of her brow and cheeks as they caught the glow of the morning sun. She reminded him of his mother in her final days. That proud beauty laid low by age and illness. A faint smile crossed his lips as he remembered his mother, so lovely when he was a boy. He had never met another to equal her. Would she be proud of him? He had kept his promise to her. He painted the beauties of the Court; his client list was extensive and illustrious, and his purity . . .

The flower seller offered a posy to a passerby and grinned. Even from where John sat, the seller's blackened, rotten teeth were clearly visible. He shuddered and turned away, his study of her face ruined by the spectacle of her teeth. He gazed up at the changing sky then at the magnificent carvings high on the church facade. The growing light caressed the intricate renditions of saints and decorative flourishes. John watched the shapes of the stone gargoyles emerge as the light brightened. The arch of their wings echoed the arch of the windows high up on the church wall, delighting him with the symmetry.

His coffee went cold, but he didn't notice, lost as he was in contemplation. When his view finally returned to the ground, he spotted the familiar shuffling figure of Henri Desjardins, no doubt still on the streets after a night of carousing.

"Desjardins! You are out early this morning. Would you care to join me for a coffee?"

The man squinted at him from under bushy eyebrows. "Is it absolutely necessary for you to expostulate so very loudly at this extremely early hour, *mon frère*?"

John glanced around at the patio but it was still empty of other patrons. He still found it awkward when Desjardins referred to their relationship. John hadn't known he had a brother until after his mother died. His father never mentioned his first wife or their son, Henri, although he and Henri had exchanged letters for years when John was a child.

Henri drew closer and leaned heavily on the wrought iron railing next to John's table then rubbed his face and yawned. John noted the white of his teeth contrasting with his dark brown skin, so different from his own coloring. No-one would imagine that they were brothers.

"Perhaps I will join you," Henri said, circling the railing. "However, unlike good Puritan boys such as yourself who did not stay up late in the arms of a beautiful woman, I have need of sustenance beyond coffee. Since you were so kind to offer." He slumped heavily into the seat opposite John who sat silent, feeling a flush cross his cheeks.

"Gracious me," Henri said. "Have I shocked you with mention of my amorous adventures? After all the years you have spent in my fair city, you have not grown accustomed to our ways?"

"Henri, you exaggerate. Not all Parisians are as profligate as you. You give us artists a bad reputation. Some of us remain pure and focus on the beauty of our art."

"Pfft, pray refrain from lecturing me this early, *mon cher*. My head is still throbbing from the excess of my indulgences, and me still without a drop of coffee. Where is that waiter?" He scanned the patio, and waved imperiously at the waiter, who hastened to his side to take his order. John raised an eyebrow. He had waited and waited for service, watching the rising sun chase the shadows from the church facade when he had arrived.

"However did you manage to get that waiter to notice you?" he asked. Henri shrugged.

"He can tell I am a Parisian, unlike yourself, mon frère. You are too obviously American."

"What? How on Earth can he tell that?"

"John, it is ineffable. Mysterious. Parisians just know other Parisians. Besides, I get my bread from his grandmother, so he has probably seen me at the bakery."

John shook his head, amused despite himself. Henri's food arrived and he attacked it with gusto, slathering mounds of butter and jam on his toasted baguette before shoving it into his mouth. John glanced away and sipped his cold coffee. Henri grimaced and gestured at John with a hunk of bread, catching his eye.

"Do you know, I've heard that French bread used to have flavor, that we were famous for it. Now, it tastes like paper."

"Really? I never noticed. It just tastes like bread."

Henri's eyebrows shot up.

"It lacks intensity, depth. Our Parisian food is bland. The Scientists don't let us starve but their food lacks flavor. Have you ever had real farmhouse butter? Butter made by hand, without machines? Isabelle gets it from her cousin sometimes. It's glorious." His eyes were dreamy. John chuckled.

"So what have you been painting? Anything worthwhile? Or more of those frowsy women you pick up off the streets?" John asked, watching Henri take another huge bite.

John could hear the smile in Henri's voice when he responded, mouth full of the despised bread.

"Those frowsy women are real, living people, John, not like the mannequins you are so fond of painting. My subjects are full of heart and substance; you can feel the life exuding from them. Well, maybe *you* cannot."

John took another sip from his cup of cold coffee. "My portraits are full of pure beauty, Henri. My commissions come from the highest ranks of French society."

Henri waved his jam-smeared knife in dismissal, before answering with a mouth half-full of toast. “Pure beauty? I would call it artificial beauty, all cosmetics and fripperies. Your paintings lack soul, John.”

“Soul? Is that what you see in those ugly people you like to paint? How will you ever be successful painting those subjects? The Academy will not exhibit your works and commoners cannot pay you to paint them.”

Henri shrugged. “My paintings are quite successful outside of this automaton-loving France. If the Scientists were not controlling everything, perhaps more French people would appreciate my art. When the real flesh and blood king returns, I will be sought after and respected here as well as in England.”

“Henri,” hissed John. “Do not speak so loudly of sedition. Flesh and blood king indeed. You know there are Watchers everywhere. And spies. That old flower seller could be one.” He darted a look up at the balcony above their heads but saw no Watcher sphere perched there.

Henri waved a carefree hand at John and pushed back from the table, his breakfast devoured.

“Bah. I know that old flower seller. I painted her last year.”

John stared at Henri aghast, eyes wide, mouth pursued in disgust. “You painted her? That horrible relic? Why on Earth would you want to do that? And who would buy the painting?”

“Ah, John, you do not see the life there? The character? She has seen so much.” Henri’s eyes were soft as he spoke.

John turned to study the huddled figure of the flower seller, trying in vain to see what Henri clearly could. All John saw as the woman let the sunlight caress her face was a mass of wrinkles and age spots. He shrugged and returned his attention to Henri who continued.

"She is rich with character; you can see in her face what a full life she has led. The lines and wrinkles speak of the roads she has traveled. Her portrait sold for a goodly sum to a rich Englishman. Of course, I spent it on wine and women, which is why I must now ask you to buy my breakfast. *D'accord*, I must go; my bed calls to me." With that, Henri rose, bowed and swaggered away. John had been staring, frowning, at the flower seller so missed the last thing Henri said. He watched Henri leave, and then realized he'd left him with the bill.

Again.

Sighing, John pulled out his billfold and paid the check.

ꟗ Φ ꟗ

Henri slouched along the street, his head aching from too much wine and not enough sleep. Despite the breakfast he had purloined from John, he could barely focus as he passed a veteran of the recently won Franco-Prussian war. The man sat with his back against a wall, his uniform faded and tattered and his right arm lying useless in his lap. He tilted his ashen brown face up, eyes bleary, and held out his cap for change.

"Please, *m'sieur*. I need food. Just a *sou*?" Henri stopped short, the haze cleared in his surprise.

"Food? Why would you need money for food? Bread is free for all French citizens and there are soup kitchens all over for veterans such as yourself." The man cast his eyes down and a hint of shame crept across his unshaven cheeks.

"You're right, m'sieur. It's not food I need."

"Well what then?" Henri asked, impatient and yet humoring the man for reasons his addled mind couldn't name.

"Brandy," the man replied. "I need brandy to cut the pain and the noise from this useless piece of machinery." He raised his right arm with his left and his sleeve fell back to reveal an arm of metal and leather, not flesh. "It does not work anymore, just hangs there humming and whining. I cannot take it off, it just thrumbs, making my bones rattle with the sound. I cannot think, cannot sleep. The noise is driving me mad." As he spoke his eyes filled with tears. "Brandy makes the noise stop. I need the money for brandy. Please." Henri fumbled in his pockets, pulling out a few loose coins.

"I am sorry, *mon ami*, this is all I have. Myself, I am a struggling painter. Take this. Do you have somewhere you can buy your brandy? It is hard to get hold of these days." The soldier grimaced a smile.

"I have a source, someone who profits off my need. Liquor does something funny to whatever powers this mechanical burden, shuts it down for a bit. Then I can sleep."

Henri's eyes went wide. He had heard nothing about the susceptibility of Augmented people to alcohol.

"So it's easier to get drunk? Hah! That would certainly save me money!"

"All I know is that the noise from this infernal thing stops when I have a bellyful of brandy. I can finally sleep for a time before it starts up again."

"Can they do nothing for you? Can the Scientist-doctors not fix it? Or take it off?"

The soldier smiled, a bitter twist to his mouth.

"Once they discharged me from the army, they washed their hands of me. Repairing these contraptions is tricky and so only fighting men get them fixed. I am too old to fight. Useless to them. Useless like this wondrous mechanical arm of mine." He spat into the gutter and glared up at the black Watcher sphere mounted on a rooftop opposite his seat.

Henri said nothing, just reached down and patted the man's good shoulder. He slowly walked away, glancing back at the veteran. The man didn't look up.

A short while later Henri arrived at the wine merchant's shop. It was still too early for the shop to be open but Henri knew the way to the back door through the warren of alleyways. The wine merchant perched on his back step, pale face up to the sun, eyes closed.

"Edouard. Good morning to you, mon ami," Henri called. "How are you on this glorious morning?" Edouard jumped, and then scowled, narrowing his eyes in recognition.

"What do you want? Are you here to pay me? I still have not seen payment for last month's bill. You had better not be here to ask for more credit."

Henri held up his hands, placating.

"Mon ami. Please. It is such a fine morning. Let us not spoil the peace of the day by arguing." Still frowning, Edouard responded,

"It was a fine morning before your ugly face darkened my door. So are you going to pay me or are you trying to wheedle more credit?"

"Ah, Edouard, I came to tell you that I have been recommending your fine establishment to my illustrious, not to mention wealthy, clients. Have they arrived to put in their orders yet?" Henri was lying. He had seen well-dressed personages entering the shop the previous day and decided to claim credit for their patronage. Edouard hesitated.

"You have been recommending my shop to whom exactly? Your clientele is not usually among members of the court." Henri smiled slyly.

"I have clients from far and wide, mon ami. I am glad they have taken my advice."

"I did not say that. I mean, they did not mention you."

"The wealthy like to think that they are the only ones with good ideas. They do not like to admit others can give good recommendations. That matters not to me. As long as your business prospers for it."

"Well, yes. I thank you, Henri."

Henri flourished a bow. "A bottle of something respectable would be acceptable, mon ami, as a token of your appreciation."

Edouard, still frowning slightly, went inside and returned with a bottle. He wrapped it with great care in a cloth before handing it to Henri, who tucked it into a large pocket in his overcoat. They exchanged goodbyes and Henri continued his journey home.

ꙮ Φ ꙮ

The sun was above the rooftops when he finally arrived at his studio apartment and dragged himself up the twelve flights of stairs, the smell of cabbage assaulting his nostrils as always. He entered the darkened studio and grinned, pleased that he had thought to close the heavy curtains before leaving the previous evening, and sank to the divan to remove his boots. A light flared across the room as a shadowed figure lit the wall lamp. Henri started, a small cry escaping his lips.

"Who's there? Isabelle?"

The light from the lamp brightened and Henri saw that the figure was masculine, dressed in a dark cloak with a hat pulled low over his face.

"Henri Desjardins?" a voice hissed. Henri trembled and dropped his boot with a thud.

"*Oui*. Who are you? What have I done to warrant this visit? Are you from the *Police Secrète*? Are you here to arrest me?"

The figure moved closer and Henri could see his face more clearly. The man smiled down at him but it was not a cheerful smile. It was more the smile of a predator about to pounce. Henri shivered.

"No, I am not a policeman and I am not . . . here you... arrest. I have come . . . to a visit pay . . . to the esteemed French painter, Monsieur Henri Desjardins. Your fame has spread to England where my master saw and enjoyed your works of art. Himself . . . particularly enjoys the, ah, natural element in your work."

Henri wondered at his visitor's broken French before shaking his head.

"M'sieur, while I am happy to learn that my work is appreciated, I am very tired and wish to seek my bed. I bid you *adieu*."

"I beg your pardon, M'sieur Desjardins. I will not . . . you keep long from your bed but it is imperative that we speak."

Henri eyed him, noting the fine material of his cloak. This was a man of some means and a potential client.

"Very well. Let us discuss what you came here for, m'sieur . . . ?"

"You may call me Jean-Luc. My last name is not necessary."

“How very mysterious of you, Jean-Luc. As is your unannounced appearance in my studio. How did you get in, by the way?”

The man shook his head, his face impassive. “This is not important. I have my ways.”

“I see. Well, my mysterious friend Jean-Luc, you mentioned an English employer, ah, no, you said master. So you work perhaps for an English nobleman?”

“Not English. My master may live away from our beloved France but he is as French as you, *monsieur*.”

Henri raised his eyebrows. Now this was interesting. Not many French nobles lived outside of France; it was forbidden to remove French assets from the country. In fact, he knew of only one French noble family living exclusively outside of France.

“Can you mean . . . the *duc d’Orléans* ?” Henri whispered. Even the mention of Louis-Philippe, the head of the last remaining cadet branch of the Bourbons, was considered treason in France, as John had reminded him. His father, the previous *duc*, had been exiled after an attempted coup thirty years ago. Jean-Luc nodded. He too lowered his voice.

“As I said, my master greatly admires your work. Himself . . . feels that perhaps you are sympathetic to, ah, his goals, his aspirations. That perhaps you would welcome a more natural France, a return to a time before all these machines.” Henri felt the hairs on his neck raise. This was dangerous talk. Men had been imprisoned for less. He sat silently for a moment before speaking.

“M'sieur. I must admit that I am more sympathetic to the natural order of the world. You have seen my paintings. I portray life, humanity, nature. These machines we have seem somehow wrong, I mean, no, not wrong . . .” he stopped speaking, afraid to admit seditious thoughts to this stranger. This Jean-Luc could be baiting him, trying to get him to admit to treason. Jean-Luc placed a hand on Henri's shoulder. It felt reassuring somehow.

"Of course, you are afraid. France is in a state of fear, fear of the machines and the Scientists. And what about it . . . do the monarchs? Nothing. They stay in their fine palace at Versailles and hold court with a select few. They refuse to allow their cousin into France even to visit. And they allow the Scientists and their machines to rule over France. Every night, you must stay inside or be wetted with the rain they create. Their spying machines, what do you call them, Watchers? They track your movements in the street. You walk in fear of the cyborg soldiers they created."

Henri thought of the veteran with his broken mechanical arm. When the arm had functioned, it had been strong, a formidable weapon. He glanced down at Jean-Luc's hand on his shoulder, an eyebrow quirked at the familiarity. The man quickly drew his hand back. Henri sighed.

"Yes, yes, this is true. The machines are everywhere. But our King and Queen have ruled for over eighty years. France knows only them. And the Scientists give free bread to all. The French people will never reject that."

"Eighty years? That is far too long. France needs a new order, my friend. We need a natural monarch, not the Augmented ones we have now. There are many of us working towards that change." The man's face was passionate now, his hands expressive as he talked.

"I, too, would like to see that," Henri said. "But what can I do? I am just a painter." Henri rubbed his hand across his face, suddenly weary.

"Just a painter? You are the famous Henri Desjardins. Surely you have the ear of many influential clients among the nobility."

Henri shook his head, his mouth drooping with sadness. "Ah, mon ami, I think you must equate my fame in England with fame here in France. Sadly, the nobility here do not esteem my work. It reminds them too much of the real world, rather than their artificial society."

Jean-Luc seemed downcast, perhaps disappointed. His mouth tightened. "I did not realize. So you do not have access to the court at Versailles?"

"No. I paint in the gardens of Versailles since they are open to the public now. But I do not have commissions at the palace."

"I see." Jean-Luc paused, seeming to be thinking. "However, I think you still may be able to help us. You see the nobles come and go, yes?"

Henri nodded, a feeling of queasy excitement gripping his gut. What was he agreeing to?

Jean-Luc continued. "Then you may yet be of assistance. We will contact you." He moved towards the door. Henri surged off the divan toward him.

"Wait! My friend John Saylor has many clients, nobles. He is often at the Palace painting them. Perhaps he could be convinced to help us."

Jean-Luc's face stretched into a crafty grin. "Your friend paints in the Queen's presence in the Nobles' Salon?"

"I, ah, I do not know. I could inquire."

"Good. Do that. I will be in contact soon. *Adieu*, Monsieur Desjardins." And with that, Jean-Luc swept out, his dark cloak swirling about him. Henri moved to the open door. His visitor had disappeared into the gloom of the stairwell. Henri shut the door and leaned against it, shaking his head in bemusement.

Now that Jean-Luc had gone, the enormity of what Henri had agreed to sank in. Deep in thought, hobbled back across the room and sank down onto the divan. He removed his second boot at last. He lay down on the divan and pulled a rough blanket over him, but despite his headache and fatigue, he couldn't sleep.

Could I really see the end of the mechanicals ruling my country? If they were gone, would France return to her natural order? I don't even know what a natural France would look like.

Henri had lived his entire life under the rule of the Augmented monarchs and their Scientists. He imagined the rain pattering its nightly cadence on the rooftops, as it did every night.

The scheduled night rains would cease without the machines to control them. There would be a natural rhythm to the rainfall. Rain in the day. Some days without any rain at all. Certainly that would be better?

Two

Adelaide strode into her laboratory workroom, cursing under her breath.

Yet another wretched Court banquet. What a complete waste of time. Why do they force me to attend these ridiculous events?

In the dim light, she glimpsed the figure of her most recent creation, looking like a body under its sheet. It was lying on what had once been a magnificent carved wood dining table. She turned up the lights and, in their white-blue electric glow, surveyed the bizarre amalgam of mechanical parts and elegant Palace décor that was her laboratory workroom. She smiled at the familiar sight: the damask wallpaper smudged black from an incident with a faulty igniter, the wainscoting dinged from collisions with out of control automatons. The priceless Persian carpet was littered with an assortment of broken gears and snips of wire. Soft whirring filled the expansive room, its source somewhere in the depths of the cabinets. Burnished wood and brass fittings gleamed in the light.

The smell of burnt wiring and machine grease was a balm to her jangled nerves. She was so tired of all those sickly courtiers bowing and scraping, hoping for favors, hoping to be pushed to the front of the line for Augmentations. She exhaled, relaxing, then moved into the room, dodging the wires and boxes on the scarred hardwood floor that snagged at her black skirts. Her mood shifted and she scowled at the jumbled mess.

This workroom is a mess. I thought I told Zoé to tidy up. Useless girl. Why on Earth did the Academy assign such a lazy child to me?

Adelaide sighed out a breath. At least she was back at work in her laboratory. She had no idea how many boring Court functions she would be obliged to attend as Royal Scientist Physician. She almost wished she were back in her laboratory in Sanary. Her work attire there did not include a ridiculously tight corset and miles of petticoats.

Pausing at the side of the covered figure, she placed a hand on its chest and a soft, secret smile crossed her plain face, giving it a momentary beauty.

"I will work on you later, my dear," Adelaide whispered. "Soon you will be fully functional. I promise."

The covered figure made no sound. Adelaide patted its chest and continued to an ornate writing desk tucked into a niche. She seated herself, brushed back wisps of her mousy brown hair and began jotting down notes in a large notebook. She needed to make repairs to one of the Queen's controllers. That would take time away from her scientific discovery work but if the controller failed and the actuator went awry, the Queen would not be pleased. Or able to move. Adelaide stifled a giggle at the mental image.

That is not funny, Adelaide. The Queen is your patient. You are responsible for her continued correct functioning. A faulty actuator would be terrifying for the poor woman.

Adelaide's internal lecture worked to subdue her mischievous thoughts and she continued writing her notes, stifling the urge to tinker with her work in progress lying beneath its shroud across the room.

"Madame?"

Adelaide jerked in surprise. She hadn't heard Zoé enter the laboratory. Her young assistant was standing near the figure on the table, head cocked to one side as she waited for a response. She was holding a brass sphere, glossy black oculars across its equator, leather straps hanging from it. It looked a bit like a metal octopus. The girl had a bag slung across her chest and was struggling under the weight of her burdens.

"Zoé. You startled me. What do you have there? Is another of those accursed Watchers in need of repair?"

The girl nodded in assent, shifting the weight of the Watcher sphere.

"Well, put it down; no, not there, foolish girl, over there," Adelaide directed her to a workbench. "This workroom is an absolute disaster. Did I not instruct you to tidy up?"

Zoé dropped the Watcher and her bag onto the workbench with a thump, cast a look around the room and shrugged.

"Is that not what servants are for, Madame? I have more important work to do."

Adelaide felt a flush rise to her face at the girl's arrogant reply.

"I told you to do it." Adelaide struggled to keep her tone level, calm.

The young woman stared at Adelaide, her eyes blazing

with unspoken anger. Adelaide sat at her desk and regarded her assistant with a placid face, waiting. The whirring of the machines was the only sound in the room. Finally, Zoé dropped her eyes.

"Very well, Madame Le Professeur. I will do as you . . . command."

She walked back to the table supporting the hidden figure, bending to pick up a wooden box from the floor. She slammed it onto the table, narrowly missing the form lying there. Adelaide gasped and half-stood, hand outstretched.

"Be careful! You almost hit my new automaton with that box."

"I apologize, Madame," Zoé said. Her eyes alighted on the figure and she reached for the cover. "What is it? I don't recall seeing it here yesterday."

Adelaide smirked, puffing her chest with pride.

"Leave it alone for now. It just arrived from my laboratory in Sanary. When it is complete, it will be my finest creation."

Zoé dropped her hand and glanced over at Adelaide, curiosity writ on her face. Adelaide returned to her notes, ignoring the unasked question on Zoé's face. The girl could wait for an explanation.

ꓭ Φ ꓷ

John climbed aboard the clanking, wheezing train bound for Versailles. He carried his art case against his chest. Around him, chattering, laughing Parisians also boarded, heading for a day out at the Palace Pleasure Gardens. They pushed and shoved their way past him to get seats near each other. Groups of merrymakers clustered together, sharing ripe cheeses, raw garlic, and other odoriferous food. John felt ill as the smells of food and unwashed people assaulted his nostrils. He was pushed along with the crowd until it released him, scattering into compartments. He breathed, alone for a brief moment in the train corridor.

He found a seat in a compartment opposite a couple cuddling on a bench next to a window. They were gazing into each other's eyes, smiling. John felt a sadness weighing on his chest as he sat alone, watching them. She was tidily, almost elegantly dressed, in that inexplicable way Parisiennes had of making cheap clothing look like couture. She fussed with the pleats and ruffles of what was obviously her best outfit. John briefly admired her curvaceous figure, encased in layers of whalebone and wool. The woman's companion glared at John's scrutiny and wrapped his arm possessively around her waist.

Romance always seemed to elude John. He turned away to look out of the window, trying to ignore the hollowness that had settled in his body. A sleek, clean, quiet electric-powered train full of richly-dressed courtiers sat on another track, also headed to Versailles. The courtiers weren't headed for the public gardens, John suspected, but the private gardens and the Palace, to the glittering, brilliant Court at Versailles to wait upon the Queen. He brightened a little, remembering that he too was headed for the Palace. His final sitting with the duchesse de Fronsac was today. John jerked back in his seat as the train lurched out of the station; he heard cheering from the next car.

The streets and buildings of Paris sped by and soon they were in the countryside. Rolling fields stretched off into the distance, golden with ripe wheat. The sky was a brilliant blue above the fields. It is almost the color of the duchesse de Fronsac's gown, John thought. He contemplated the scenery, the sight soothing him, until a voice interrupted his reverie. It was the conductor, collecting tickets. John silently held out his ticket, still staring out of the window, but the man didn't take the hint. He began chatting to John, the couple opposite and anyone else in range of his booming voice.

"Are you off to the Pleasure Gardens alone, mon ami? Oh, oh, oh! Perhaps you are meeting your sweetheart there? Ah, romance! It is indeed a fine day for picnicking and the like. Heh heh. I would like to be there myself . . . with my dear wife of course, but alas! I must do my duty and remain on this train. Someone must transport the good people of Paris to their merriment." John responded with a brief twist of his lips, his ticket outstretched, tamping down his loneliness.

The conductor continued to expound, his thumbs stuck in the pockets of his waistcoat.

"Strange times are upon us, my good people. Have you heard about the mysterious, swirling, black cloud in Normandy? I was told by the best authority that an enormous funnel came down to Earth and tore a house to pieces with the ferocity of its wind."

John's interest was piqued and he turned from the window to ask, "Was it really some sort of funnel cloud? I thought those were unheard of here in France with the weather controlling machines in place." A triumphant smile spread across the conductor's face as he captured John's interest.

"Ah yes, that is what the Scientists are calling it, a funnel cloud. Seems that one of the weather machines was not working properly and caused some unusual weather. A whole house, on the outskirts of a village. Torn to pieces. Can you imagine?"

The conductor paused but clearly had more to say. The woman opposite sat up, and interjected.

"It has been fixed now. *Presidente Le Scientist* said so in the newspaper. He said that there was nothing to be concerned about." Finished with her demonstration of knowledge, the woman lapsed into silence and laid her head on her beau's shoulder. He smoothed down her hair and tightened his arm around her. The conductor glanced at the woman, his eyebrows raised, as if waiting for more, then turned back to John and took his ticket.

"Well, good day to you, sir. I hope your lady love is still waiting for you." With a wink, he exited the compartment. John exhaled with relief and returned to contemplating the passing scenery. The colors and textures of the autumnal fields calmed him. He considered pulling out his art case and sketching the passing scene, but the movement of the train lulled him into a dreamy stillness.

A short time later, they arrived outside the village of Versailles. Within a few moments, the huffing, hissing train screeched to a halt at the small, immaculately-kept station.

John got off the train, his art case cradled protectively against his chest as his fellow passengers jostled and bustled past him. Couples strolled past him holding hands, linking arms, wrapping arms around waists. None spared him a glance as he stood next to the train, watching them all leave. Across the platform, courtiers disembarked from the graceful electric train John had spotted earlier. He moved closer and peered in through a window, noticing how light sparkled off the silver and crystal goblets on a table inside. A pair of chic women, with intricate hairstyles and perfectly smooth complexions sat there, heads together and whispering. A waiter hovered nearby, looking anxious to finish clearing the table but unwilling to disturb them. John stood scrutinizing the women, enjoying their porcelain beauty. Two men in Court dress swept past him, one declaring to his companion,

"*Pouah*! How I detest sycophants, peeping in on our private affairs. Why can the station police not move him along?"

"Give him no mind, Antoine, he is too, too pathetic," replied his companion. John stiffened and turned away from the window, flushing with humiliation at being caught peeping. The men had moved past him so didn't see him glower after them, clenching his fists. John's heart beat hard and he felt overheated. His fellow passengers were hurrying away through the station, faces alight with anticipated pleasure, skirts and picnic baskets brushing against him. No-one spared him a look as he stood there, clutching his art case to his breast. John slung his case over his shoulder and forced himself to move.

He walked slowly along the now-deserted platform, struggling to calm himself before exiting the station. John had planned to take a hired carriage to the Palace but as he surveyed the road in front of the station, the sneering courtiers entered the last carriage at the station and the vehicle pulled away, steaming and rattling.

John sighed deeply and hoisted the leather strap of his art case higher onto his shoulder. The sun was high in the sky, blindingly bright in the perennially clear blue sky. The weather machines seemed to be operational here. A crowd of singing, laughing holidaymakers paced him as he walked along the dusty country road. He shifted his eyes away from them and gazed at the golden fields flanking the road, wheat stalks swaying in the breeze. Two rough-looking men yelled mock insults at each other next to John. His ears rang with their shouts. He winced and walked faster to move away from them, only to come up behind a gaggle of young women in gaudy dresses shrieking with laughter. He intercepted a few interested looks and blown kisses from the women and dropped his gaze.

Henri would be thrilled to be strolling with them. His so-called real women. They must think I have money to spend on them at the Pleasure Gardens. Have a little fun at my expense, then go home and forget me. I'll find my pure love someday and then Henri can keep his painted pea hens to himself.

Tightening his mouth, he refused to raise his eyes to acknowledge them. The grey dust from the dirt road coated his previously shiny black shoes as he trudged along. He grimaced. The Queen preferred a rustic atmosphere around Versailles so she would not allow the roads to be paved. Now he would arrive at the Palace looking travel-worn and those damned courtiers would have more reason to sneer and look down their long aristocratic noses at him.

The ornate gilded iron gates of the gardens loomed ahead. John was warm in his wool suit and was sure his face glowed red with exertion. He spoke briefly to the sentry at the gate. The officer checked for his name on a list and waved him through the entrance for the private gardens reserved for the aristocracy. All was quiet and calm inside this part of the gardens. The overhanging trees cooled the air and John inhaled their fresh smell. A group of court ladies strolled by, their skirts rustling, trains dragging across the well-groomed gravel pathway. They spoke softly to one another.

How different they are from those chattering magpies in the public gardens.

He smiled and sketched a bow as they passed him.

None deigned to notice. John's smile faltered. He continued on and at last reached the Palace, circling the grand edifice to a side wing, to one of the servants' entrances. It led directly to the servants' hall.

A chambermaid sat at a long oaken table, polishing a baroque silver candelabrum. She glanced up as he entered the room and a huge grin split her round little face.

"Monsieur Saylor! How good it is to see you! 'Ave you come to paint *la belle duchesse*?"

John nodded in response. "Bon jour, Jeanne, you are well, I hope? Although it seems that Gerard has once again convinced you to do his work." John gestured towards the silver arrayed on the table in front of her. Jeanne waved her hand nonchalantly at the silver.

"Pfft. I do not mind polishing silver. It keeps me from cleaning out pisspots in the bedchambers of those randy gentlemen."

John pursed his lips and shook his head. "Those gentlemen should keep their hands to themselves. They have no right to paw at you."

Jeanne laughed. "I just stay out of their way. I do not want to make trouble and lose my job. Do not fret about me, m'sieur. Go on and paint the beautiful lady."

"Yes, I do not wish to be late for *La Duchesse*. She would be most put out." He adopted a mock-solemn expression and Jeanne grinned cheekily back at him.

ꕤ Φ ꕤ

The duchesse de Fronsac reclined on a velvet chaise lounge in her drawing room when he entered, ushered in by one of the ubiquitous ushers of the Palace. She waved him over imperiously.

"My portrait will be finished today, *n'est ce pas*?" She drew her blonde ringlets across her shoulder and perused him from under her long dark lashes, a faint smile on her painted lips.

"Yes, Madame, I believe so." John tried not to stare at the sultry woman arranged in front of him on what was in essence a bed. She wore a loose, low-cut wrapper, the heavy blue silk clinging to her curves. An usher set up John's easel in front of the chaise lounge and carefully positioned the unfinished canvas on the easel. John murmured his thanks.

He opened his art case and took out his palette, brushes, and tubes of paint, then carefully squeezed out and mixed his colors, trying to match the paint to the duchesse's gown. Her gaze burned at him as he mixed. He tried not to pay attention but her voice shattered his concentration.

"I find I will miss our little sessions," she said, her voice low and throaty. "It is most gratifying to have you stare at me for hours, examining every detail of my face and figure. Almost as if you were my lover."

John felt the blush rise on his cheeks and swallowed before responding.

"It has been my pleasure, Madame," he mumbled, eyes on his palette. She laughed.

"Indeed? Do tell. Or are you merely flattering me?"

He stole a glance at her, wondering if she really wanted an answer. Her face was unreadable, frozen into a faint smile by the enamel painted on her face. "Painting beauty such as yours is what I dream of, *Madame La Duchesse*," he replied quietly. The noblewoman didn't respond. Perhaps she was used to receiving extravagant compliments.

John, unable to fathom the mind of the noblewoman, concentrated on his work, on the canvas in front of him. His eyes took in the perfect color of the paint on the palette and he raised his brush. Daubing paint across the canvas, John refined the image already there, bringing out highlights in the silk, deepening the shadows around her. He relaxed as he painted, focusing on the form and lines of his subject. Her dress was a rich cobalt blue and John had searched long and hard for the matching pigment. The blue of the gown made her pale skin look creamy and rich and deepened the shade of her green eyes. He looked a little closer. The makeup at her décolletage didn't quite cover the dusky hue of her skin. So the duchesse wasn't quite as pure white as the rest of Court. He carefully whitened her bosom in the painting, knowing she, like all the Court ladies, was striving to match the Queen's reputed perfect porcelain complexion. He imagined the scandal if anyone admitted to the Queen's presence was discovered to be anything other than pure white and winced to himself.

As he finished the last touches, he compared his subject with the painting and grimaced. He could see cracks in the enamel makeup around the real duchesse's mouth. He looked again at the painting to make sure that her skin was portrayed as flawless. She would not take kindly to any imperfections appearing in her portrait.

"Well? Is it complete? Have you captured my exquisite charms, my talented painter? I think perhaps this portrait will be exhibited in the Royalist Salon, if it is good enough. But mostly, I hope it pleases my husband. I must lure him back to my bed to sire a legitimate heir."

John coughed slightly, not sure of an appropriate response, and examined the portrait rather than facing the duchesse. He turned the painting to show her. She smiled her faint smile and clapped her hands.

"Yes! That will do nicely. My servant will see you out."

Her abrupt dismissal left John a bit deflated. He wondered how long it would take for her to remember to send payment for his work. That was the trouble with painting the aristocracy: they could easily afford his fees but frequently forgot to pay him. He hated having to contact their financiers for payment. It seemed so *gauche*.

John made his way back to the gardens, hoping to spend a little time in that peaceful pastoral setting. More noble ladies were promenading along the pathways now, looking like blossoms in their brightly colored gowns. Again he bowed as groups of them passed, and, as before, he was ignored, until he spotted a very young noblewoman, skipping along behind three ladies. They locked eyes and she smiled before looking away, a slight flush appearing on her pale cheeks.

She would be worth painting.

His eyes lingered on her delicate features and soft, unpainted skin. She wore a plain white silk gown and her dark hair lay heavily against her slender neck in a simple chignon. John had a sudden longing to lift the heavy mass of hair from her neck and kiss her there. Dismayed by his reaction to her, he shifted his eyes away but then heard a cry. Turning back, he saw the young girl sway, then sink to the ground in a puddle of white silk. She lay unconscious while court ladies twittered around her. John stood rooted to the spot as people rushed to and fro around him. An army of ushers moved in and scooped up the unconscious girl, and then a short woman in unrelieved black pushed past the crowd. She directed the servants to carry the girl away into the Palace. John frowned as he watched them take her away.

Why would she just collapse like that? She had seemed so

young and vibrant.

He watched as a pair of noblewoman swayed past him, arms linked and a riot of silk ruffles and pleats adorning each of them. John never tired of looking at their perfect forms.

The ladies of the Court, in an effort to produce the fashionable silhouette, often tightened their corsets too much. They made great sacrifices to create that loveliness. John had heard that they even fainted sometimes. The girl was young and her maid had probably overtightened her corset.

Remembering again the scene, a thought occurred to him.

Who was that woman in black who took away the girl? Some kind of doctor? I thought the Scientists were the only people at Court who wore all black.

John resumed his walk, rattled by what he had just witnessed and uncertain why.

ཱྀ Φ ཱྀ

The ushers carried the limp figure of Marie-Ange into the large, darkened laboratory off the checkered main hallway of the Palace. Heavy curtains obscured tall windows on the far side of the room and the air hung still.

"Lay her down here," Adelaide said as she cleared metal tools off a long table with a clatter. "Watch her head, you clumsy oaf!" she rebuked as the ushers stumbled around in the dim light and jostled Marie-Ange.

"Your pardon, Madame Le Professeur," one murmured. They laid her gently on the table and stepped back, bowing to the diminutive Scientist Physician. Marie-Ange lay surrounded by her skirts and petticoats, as if she had collapsed into a snowdrift. Despite the jostling she had still not regained consciousness. Adelaide bit her lip and scrutinized the frail girl. The ushers hovered nearby. Noticing them, she yelled, "Out! Out of my laboratory!"

They scuttled out, Adelaide following to close the door as soon as they were through it. Returning to Marie-Ange's side, she turned a knob on a lantern by the table, which glowed with a blue-white light. She placed the lantern next to the girl's head before moving across the dark, cluttered room to turn on another of the brilliant lights. As the light brightened, Adelaide dodged around the wooden cabinets and wires then swore as she banged her shin against a metal box on the hardwood floor.

Zut! How many time to I have to tell that wretched Zoé to tidy up?

Adelaide opened an elaborately carved wooden cabinet and rummaged noisily around inside.

"Where is the blasted thing?" she muttered to herself, leaning further into the confines of her tool cabinet. After several moments, she popped out holding a large leather bag. The contents of the bag shifted and clanked together as she hefted it back to Marie-Ange's side.

Adelaide pulled a listening tube out of the bag and pressed one end to the girl's chest, and the other end to her own ear. She listened for a few seconds and cursed softly. With quick movements, Adelaide unfastened Marie-Ange's bodice and pressed the listening tube to the girl's bared chest. The ugly puckered scar seemed to stare up at Adelaide from between Marie-Ange's small breasts.

"Ah faint, so faint," she spoke softly. "Your precious heart is not beating as it should, *ma chère*." Adelaide retrieved a small box-like brass device from her bag and laid it on the girl's chest over the scar. The device hummed with a steady rhythm.

Marie-Ange drew a deep breath and exhaled loudly, beginning to cough. Adelaide removed the box from the girl's chest and closed her bodice. Marie-Ange opened her eyes and gazed up at Adelaide, fear and confusion warring on her face.

"Madame Le Professeur. What happened?" Her voice was faint and husky. Adelaide took Marie-Ange's hand and tried to smile.

"Ma chère, you fainted in the garden. Your heart was not behaving itself. Have you been overexerting? I have warned you to take care. You are too delicate to run and skip and dance as I know you would like to do."

Marie-Ange nodded. Shame darkened her face, but only for an instant. "Oh, Madame Le Professeur, I was just so excited to finally be here at Court. The gardens are so magnificent; I wanted to see all of the statuary and the fountains." She paused and frowned, her mouth a delicate *moue*. "I suppose I did too much walking."

"The gardens are quite extensive, ma chère. Even a healthy young woman would be hard-pressed to visit them all in one afternoon." Adelaide harrumphed and shook her head. "Perhaps it was not wise of your parents to send you here. There is too much temptation to overexert yourself and they do not have enough control over you. I will speak to Her Majesty about keeping you close by her side."

Marie-Ange's face fell. "Oh no, Madame Le Professeur! You know Her Majesty never walks in the gardens. I would never see them."

"Marie-Ange, we must keep you healthy. I do not know what we could do for you if your heart should fail. What if you trip and fall? You know your heart is delicate and a fall could be very dangerous to you. I may have to recommend the Queen sends you back to Aix-en-Provence."

Marie-Ange tried to sit up at that, tears welling in her eyes. "No, no, please do not send me home. I have only just arrived and there is so much to see and do."

Adelaide frowned and shook her head, pushing Marie-Ange back down onto the table. "That is precisely the problem. The temptation is too great here."

Marie-Ange turned her face away, frowning. "I don't care. I will not return home. I will assure Her Majesty that I will be careful. She will not send me away if I tell her how much it means to me to serve her here at Court. You have no control over this. I am not going back to Aix-en-Provence." She paused, and took a deep breath. "Please send in my maidservants, Madame Le Professeur. I wish to return to my rooms."

"But you must stay still," Adelaide interjected, trying to catch the girl's eye.. Marie-Ange continued to look away.

"I wish to rest in my rooms. I will summon you if I need your further assistance, Madame Le Professeur."

Adelaide sniffed at the haughty dismissal, then stalked to the door to call to the ushers who stood waiting outside.

"Fetch Mademoiselle de Laincel's maidservants, then assist her back to her suite." Adelaide stood silently fuming next to the door.

The little imbecile. Ridiculous, silly nincompoop. How dare she risk her life for a bit of Court gaiety?

She rubbed her forehead and tried to quell her anger, to little avail. The maidservants arrived after what seemed like an eternity of silence. Astonishing how the girl could keep up her fit of pique.

She must truly detest her home in Aix-en-Provence if she

was willing to risk her health to stay at Court.

In a flurry of activity, the ushers carried Marie-Ange from the room. The girl still refused to speak or even look at Adelaide. After they had left, Adelaide turned off the lights and departed, locking her laboratory-workroom.

I'll go for a walk in the public gardens. The roses are still blooming. I need a little time to myself, away from these unreasonable nobles.

Three

Henri lounged in the Café Guerbois, his back against the plaster wall so he could see everyone entering. The steaming cup of coffee in front of him gave off a rich, toasted scent. He savored the smell, breathing deeply before picking up the heavy white porcelain cup. He sipped the hot, bitter liquid slowly, closing his eyes. Henri adored good, strong coffee, just like his *grandmère* used to make. Isabelle never got it quite right. A cold spray of droplets hit him in the face, jarring him out of his reverie. He opened his eyes, frowning, and saw John standing next to him brushing rain drops off the shoulders of his wool jacket. His brother's nose was pink with cold. John didn't seem to notice Henri's irritated look. His face had a distracted look on it and he was peering out the window.

"*Bonjour*, Henri. Did you know that it is actually raining out there? In broad daylight? What on Earth is going on?"

Henri shrugged, unconcerned.

"It happens sometimes. Perhaps one of the Scientists turned the wrong lever or some such."

"I suppose so. The weather seems very unsettled. Did

you hear that a great funnel cloud touched down near Normandy?"

Henri raised an eyebrow at that. "Huh. A tornado? That is quite an unusual occurrence. My *grandmère* used to tell me of the many tornados she saw when she was a young girl. But we do not see them much since the machines took over our weather."

"So what is happening? Do you think the machines have stopped working?"

"Ah, that would be lovely. To have real weather? I am enjoying the rain clouds today. One does get tired of the constant, unchanging sunlight." Henri smiled dreamily, eyes unfocused as he mused, but still he could see John's face seemed troubled, his forehead wrinkled as if in thought.

"But Henri, if the weather machines fail, there could be droughts or floods. The crops could fail as they do in other places where the weather is erratic. France has been immune to famine since the weather control machines were invented. If France's weather changed for the worse, it would be all the talk in America, I can tell you that. If my countrymen knew about the weather machines . . . "

Henri gazed up at John still standing next to him and murmured, "Yes, there could be droughts and famines. And hungry people do not suffer incompetent rulers."

John's eyes widened. "Hush, Henri. You could be thrown into the Bastille for speaking like that." He glanced away from Henri and a sudden smile lit his face. Henri followed his eyes and spotted a slight, dapper man approaching.

"Arthur!" John's voice rang out in the close space of the cafe. "You're here! It's so good to see you, my friend."

This new man smiled, returning John's greeting quietly,

Henri noted. The men shook hands and then the new arrival turned to Henri.

"You must be the famous Henri Desjardins. It is an honor to meet you, sir. John has written me much about you."

Henri couldn't help but laugh his booming laugh and stood to clasp hands with Arthur. "Famous? Me? That is too kind of you, m'sieur. But I must know, what abominable tales has our mutual friend been telling you? No doubt they are true!" Arthur gave a noticeable wince at Henri's exuberance but answered with a wavering smile.

The men all seated themselves and Henri waited while the others ordered coffees. As they waited, Henri asked Arthur, "You have newly arrived from America, have you not? Shocking the stories I hear from there. It is well that you are safe here in France. And I think John has told me you are attending Gleyre's teaching studio? A fine teacher; that was a good choice you made. Do you know he taught me when I first came to Paris? Ah, those were carefree days. . . " Henri trailed off and Arthur interjected,

"Yes, I have been in Paris a few short months. It is a magnificent city. And Monsieur Gleyre is very kind to me. He is most encouraging."

"And why would he not be kind and encouraging? You pay his fees!" Henri guffawed at his own joke.

John spoke up then, his voice full of reproach. "Henri, you must understand that American art circles are not accepting of artists of African descent. Arthur has been painting seriously for several years now but has been unable to succeed in America merely because of his skin color."

Henri's faced turned serious and he shook his head, eyeing Arthur. "I am sorry to hear that, Arthur. I think you will find yourself much more at home here in Paris. We

French do not judge people that way. Well, except for the nobility but they're hidden away at Versailles mostly and we don't have to endure them." At that, he twisted his mouth in a sour grimace. "You or I will never be allowed to paint them. My brother is allowed admittance to their rarefied circles because he can pass." Henri watched as Arthur swiveled his head to look at John who flushed at the attention.

"John? You and Henri are brothers? So you have African ancestry also? I had no idea," Arthur said, his thin eyebrows raised.

"I am not proud that in order to receive noble commissions, I must deny my heritage," John stated, not making eye contact with Arthur.

"But—I don't understand—why is it so important to you to paint these nobles? What is it about them that demands your attention?" Arthur asked.

Henri snorted and answering for John, said, "John feels that the pinnacle of true beauty is to be found in the French Court. All those enameled pure white faces and delicate noses. And since he only wishes to paint beauty, he must go to Court." John glared at Henri but said nothing.

Arthur studied John for several long moments then said, "How limited."

John glared back, a defiant tilt to his chin, but he didn't respond. The men sat in silence. Henri tried to cover up the awkwardness by addressing Arthur.

"Arthur, what do you paint? Which painters do you admire?"

"I am partial to Manet—" he began before Henri interrupted.

"Manet! Yes! I agree; Manet is absolutely brilliant. I am particularly partial to the authenticity with which he depicted Parisian life. Don't you agree?"

Arthur nodded and began to speak but Henri continued.

"His subjects seem so real, so alive. I strive for that level of authenticity. He shows what is truly there, rather than what one believes to be true."

Henri cast a sideways look at John, who sat staring into his coffee, stonily silent.

Arthur spoke up, his face alight with a restrained passion, "I too wish to show what is real. I believe that one must paint people in settings natural to them, rather than in some sort of tableau. That seems more true to me. I wish to portray the truth."

"As do I," John murmured. Arthur and Henri both turned to John, waiting for him to elaborate. He did not continue his thought. Henri grew tired of waiting and asked John, "So what lovely noblewoman are you painting now, John?" Henri asked. John smiled, and dropped his eyes briefly. Henri was intrigued.

Why he looks almost coy. I wonder if he has seduced her.

"I have just completed a portrait of the duchesse de Fronsac. She is indeed quite lovely," John replied. Henri noticed a slight flush across John's cheeks and grinned broadly, his suspicions confirmed.

"And? Does she find you quite handsome?" he asked with a teasing tone. John laughed, a short, sudden laugh.

"Oh, perhaps. She certainly is talkative."

"Yes? And does she do more than talk and pose?" Henri asked. Arthur appeared to have finally grasped the gist of the conversation and seemed shocked, his eyes wide.

"She is a married woman, is she not? Surely she would not welcome improper advances?" Both John and Henri laughed at Arthur's naiveté and Henri responded, "She is a member of the French nobility. As long as she is discreet, she can do more than welcome advances, improper or otherwise. My question to John is does she welcome his advances? Or is she the sort of woman who makes her own?"

"Henri! You know I do not indulge in dalliances with my clients. I would not risk my career for the transient pleasures of an illicit *affaire*."

"Not even with the lovely ones? Not even the welcoming, lovely ones with distant husbands?" John shook his head, but Henri noticed the smile that curled one corner of his friend's mouth.

"She is married, Henri. I can restrain myself. But I saw someone at Versailles . . . "

Henri noticed that Arthur had stopped paying attention. He was instead staring out of the window, a haunted look on his face. John and Henri craned their necks to see what he was watching. Out in the street, a troop of policemen had stopped and were speaking to a man sitting on the pavement in the pouring rain. The man was dressed in a faded, torn uniform, its grey color echoed by his greyed ochre skin. His eyes were wide as he stared up at the men looming above him. Henri noticed his useless arm lying in his lap and recognized him as the veteran with the broken mechanical arm. Henri's handout hadn't lasted him long. He was back on the streets, begging money for brandy again. Only this time, the police had noticed him. Henri winced when he saw one of the police kick at the seated veteran. The heavy boot landed on the man's side and his face twisted in a rictus of pain. Another of the assailants reached down and dragged the thin, bedraggled man to his feet. The policeman appeared to be shouting into his face. All of a sudden, he let go of the veteran's arm, who staggered back against the wall behind him. The policeman's arm started spasming and jerking. The other four policemen watched in alarm as his other arm started flailing around as well. The look of horror on the man's face as he lost control of his arms was apparent even from inside the cafe.

Henri muttered, "It must be the rain. They can't get those mechanical Augmentations too wet." Henri caught John's surprised look and continued. "Did you ever wonder why you don't see the Augmented police at night? They can't be out in the rain. It buggers up the machinery."

Outside, the troop of police marched off quickly, supporting their malfunctioning colleague as they went. The beleaguered veteran slumped back down on to the pavement, head in his hand.

Arthur finally spoke up, "So much for a society that does not treat its people of color disrespectfully."

"What do you mean?" Henri asked, lifting his eyebrows and staring at Arthur.

"You saw what I saw, did you not? Those white policemen were harassing the beggar because of his skin color."

"What? No, he was begging. Begging is illegal in Paris, Arthur. The police often come by and arrest the beggars. I don't think that had anything to do with his skin color."

"Oh no? How many pure white beggars do you see? It could be racially-inspired harassment."

"Pure white beggars? My dear Arthur, so few of us Parisians are pure white. Unlike your America. And if we were in your America the police would be more likely to harass beggars because of the color of their skin. But the police in France don't harass people of color randomly. They instead harass those who speak out against the monarchy." The café had gone oddly silent, and Henri's words seemed to echo. Henri could not ignore the hard look John gave him.

Sipping his coffee, Henri swallowed the words he'd nearly spoken and instead gazed back at the veteran beggar on the street.

ഌ Φ ഌ

Later that evening, John sat nursing a glass of burgundy waiting for Henri to arrive, his body tense. As the sun set, a chill settled over the bustling patio of the Bistro de Royales. John shivered, but quickly stiffened again. He still felt defensive after his coffee with Arthur and Henri. He had hoped that his friends would get along, but he hadn't expected to feel like the outsider as a result.

The people around him chattered and preened, showing off their finery. John drank in the scene faster than his wine, looking at an elaborate chignon here, a delicate hand there. The well-dressed women around him didn't seem to notice him in his plain, dark suit, perhaps thinking him a businessman rather than an artist longing to paint their lovely faces.

At last, Henri arrived, his usual swagger commanding a second look from more than one of the nobles crowding the patio.

"Ah, John, greetings and how do you fare this fine evening?" He sat down and imperiously commanded the waiter to his side.

"What is that," he said, looking at John's glass. "Burgundy?"

John merely nodded as Henri turned his attention to the waiter. "I'll have a glass, too, and some escargots and perhaps some of that fresh Brie you have hiding in the back. Oh, and a beefsteak." Finished with his order, he turned to John. "It's good to see you again so soon, mon frère. To what do I owe the honor of your much-welcomed invitation to sup at this fine establishment?"

John stared at Henri for a moment, taking in his brother's relaxed demeanor.

Should I bring up the coffee date? It seems petty now. I'm probably being immature.

Shaking off his sulkiness, he drew a breath.

"Henri? I need your advice. I saw this woman at Versailles—"

Henri interrupted, "Oh ho, the famously celibate John Saylor has finally found a lady love? Do tell!" The waiter arrived with the wine and Henri took it with a smile.

John felt a flush surge across his face and he stammered a little. "No, no, it is not . . . um, not exactly. She is, well, she is a noblewoman, very young," he said, feeling his face soften as he pictured the girl. "And she's very beautiful. Her skin is magnificent, like a gardenia, pale and smooth. Not painted, though. She is free of cosmetics. Henri, her freshness stands out among the others there at Court."

Henri smiled, and sipped his wine. "She sounds lovely. But John, a noble at Court? And unmarried? She is unattainable for the likes of you and me. Best you aspire to loving someone more of our station. Someone to keep your bed warm is what you need, mon frère, not a high-born delicate flower."

John shook his head, frowning. "Henri! She is much too young for me to think about in that way! It is her beauty that captivated me. I want to paint her."

"Ah, I see. So you want a commission to paint this lovely young blossom." Henri sat back in his chair. John nodded, sitting forward, his face lit up.

"Yes, exactly. I know that if I paint her, the Royalist artists will adore it and I will be exhibited prominently at the next Salon."

Henri groaned and swirled the wine in his glass, watching it for a moment before responding. "John, why do you care so much what the Royalists thinks of your work?" He darted a quick look around. A Watcher sphere sat on the awning above them, an ominous red light blinking from its interior, Henri leaned closer to John, dropping his voice. "You know the Royalists are just a flock of old chickens, clucking about a ruffle on some courtier's dress," he whispered. "The paintings in their Salon are meaningless, barely worthy of being called art. The Royalist artists are old-fashioned, stagnant, beyond boring, mon frère. They simply have no soul." He slumped into his chair and gazed across at a table of chattering nobles, who appeared oblivious to the conversation.

John leaned back and crossed his arms. He frowned across the table at Henri. "Soul! Henri, once again, you lecture me about your obsession with the soul. It is beauty that I aspire to. If my paintings are not full of beauty, who would want to look at them?"

Henri shook his head sadly and finished his wine. "John, you're missing the point. Art is not all about popularity; it's about expressing yourself, showing the world your vision, your reflection of it. There is more to art than beauty."

"So art should show all the ugliness and flaws in the world? Like your paintings of that wrinkled apple of a flower seller? Bah! No-one wants an unpleasant painting hanging in their home. That is why you are not successful with your art and have to sponge off your friends." Henri slammed his empty wine glass on the table.

"Once again, you are wrong, John. Misguided and shallow. Many people outside of France adore my paintings. I am not attempting to make a fancy decoration for a fancy house with my art. I do not flatter my clients with pretty little pictures of their pretty little faces. I am trying to show life, real life, not a shallow depiction of ephemeral beauty."

"Shallow?" John inhaled sharply. He pushed his chair back from the table abruptly and stood. "I would rather be shallow, Henri Desjardins, than wallow in the dregs of society." He threw some bills on the table and walked away, leaving Henri sitting at the table, glaring after him.

ꕥ Φ ꕥ

As he walked, John's anger drained away and he regretted his impetuous words. Henri was not just his brother; he was his oldest friend in Paris. He had been a rock for him to lean on after the death of his mother. John remembered his shock at discovering their relationship when he read Desjardins' letters to his father . . . their father. Henri Desjardins, a real painter. And his half-brother. The night rain began, a steady shower that penetrated his wool jacket as he strode through the streets of Montmartre. It was Henri who had introduced him to his master, Gleyre, and other influential painters in Paris. Without him, John would still be struggling for his *entrée* into Parisian artistic circles. For all that Henri disdained the rich clients that John craved, he knew enough of them to be able to recommend the young John Saylor when he was first attempting to build his career. John wouldn't be able to buy Henri dinner now without that help years ago.

He winced as he recalled throwing the money down on the table, as if he were paying off an unwelcome debt. John owed so much to Henri. Far more than a simple dinner could ever repay.

He arrived home, drenched to the skin, and slumped shivering, into an armchair in his cold, dark sitting room.

What will I do if Henri washes his hands of me after this? Have I destroyed my friendship with him? How could I be such an ass to my only brother?

He groaned, remembering his contemptuous words and sat alone, watching the pouring rain through the window, regret eating at him.

ꟈ Φ ꟈ

The rain had stopped when John stepped into his studio. He was cold and a sad dullness filled him. The high ceilings echoed back his footsteps, emphasizing the emptiness of the room. He pulled back the heavy curtains from the window, letting the moonlight flood in. He noted the contrast between the pure white light and the shadows in the room without emotion. The usual thrill and urge to paint the image was absent. He stood still for a moment then spotted a brush that had dropped onto the floor. John picked it up and put it back on his easel. It still had paint encrusted in the bristles so he picked it back up and took it to the small sink in the corner of the room. He pumped to get the water flowing from the tap, then washed the brush slowly, unconsciously. Memories of the evening flooded back in and he gripped the brush, growing angry again.

That damn Desjardins. Why does he think he can talk to me like that? Because he's my older brother? Why do I put up with him? He may be a talented painter but so am I. He has no right to judge me. Shallow? How dare he call my work shallow? Does he not understand the way my heart sings when I create a beautiful painting?

He paced the room as he went over the fight with Henri in his head. He stopped in the middle of the room as a wave of loneliness hit him.

But without Henri, I have no friends and no family. My mother is gone. I have no lover. All I have is my art and what is that? Is it a shallow attempt at creating beauty? Is Henri right?

John's musings were interrupted when he noticed a white envelope on the floor near the door. His housekeeper must have slipped it under the door while he was out. Curious, he bent to pick up the envelope, noting its heavy, expensive paper. It was addressed to him and when he flipped it over, saw a seal on the back. Many of his noble clients used grand seals on their envelopes but this wasn't one he recognized. Perhaps it was payment or a new commission? Shaken out of his melancholy, he fetched a letter opener and carefully slit open the envelope. John drew out the thick paper within and took it over to the window to read it. It too was heavy, expensive, high quality paper. Lines of precise penmanship in deep, dark ink filled the page. His hands shook as he realized the letter was from the Palace, from the Queen's Secretary. It was indeed a new commission.

"You are requested to attend upon Her Majesty, Queen Marie Thérèse, at the Palace of Versailles in order to execute a portrait of Her Majesty—" John stopped reading with a gasp. Could this be real? Was he dreaming? Was he actually being commissioned to paint a portrait of the Queen of France? He began to shake and sat down on a stool by the window. It creaked alarmingly; it was more a prop for his paintings than an actual functioning piece of furniture. He ignored the complaining seat and lifted the missive closer to his face. The stark black letters leapt up at him.

Yes. That was his name on the letter. The Queen had

commissioned him.

He wondered briefly how he had come to her notice. One of his courtier clients was the most likely candidate, but which one?

Smiling to himself, John remembered the flirtatious duchesse de Fronsac. She had been so pleased with her portrait and she was one of the Queen's ladies-in-waiting. It must have been her. Perhaps he should send her flowers to thank her, with a note. Ah, but what of her husband? He might be offended by another man sending his wife flowers. Or did the ladies of the court receive flowers from men who were not their husband without censure? He shook his head. The workings of the court were still a mystery to him, despite his portfolio of noble clients.

John rubbed his face, grimacing a little at the bristles on his cheeks. The missive in his hand drew his attention once more and he read further. He was to appear at Court the day after tomorrow at 10am promptly. His brow furrowed at the time. That seemed much too early for Court ladies to be receiving, especially the Queen. He had heard talk about some sort of complex rising and dressing ritual that tradition obliged the Queen to follow, but he wasn't sure about the timing. He stood up and began pacing, hitting the letter against his hand as he walked.

The Queen of France. He was to paint the Queen of France.

John began trembling again, his stomach tight and twisting.

Oh God, I hope I do not have to paint her in déshabillée. No, surely, this will be a formal state portrait. That would be awkward, seeing a monarch in a state of undress.

John felt his cheeks grow warm at the thought. He tried

to recall seeing a portrait of Queen Marie Thérèse but one had not been made public in the entire time he had lived in France. He calculated and came up with seventeen years, at least, since the public had seen a depiction of their Queen. The people of France were waiting to see it, a portrait he was now responsible for creating. This painting could ensure his reputation in the Royalist Salon, and in France. If he were to successfully complete it.

John walked over to his larger-than-life portrait of a society lady, the one that had caused such a scandal. He scrutinized it. Could he create a painting that all of France would love? Or would his painting once again be rejected by the Salon? The Queen was purported to be a great beauty. The noblewomen he painted claimed to be emulating the elaborate hairstyles and pure white *maquillage* of the Queen. It should be easy for John to create a flattering painting. But what if his portrait did not please Her Majesty? And then what if they all disdained him for not portraying their Queen in a pleasing fashion? What if he was unsuccessful with this commission?

John walked to the window and peered out into the blackness. He saw himself failing at his life goal and lapsing into obscurity. Shuddering, he leaned against the window frame, forehead against the cold glass of the window.

Perhaps I should just refuse the commission? Perhaps it is simply too lofty for me to attempt?

But he knew that his reputation would suffer if he refused to paint the Queen. He walked to his writing desk. With hands still shaking, he lit a lamp and carefully penned his acceptance.

Four

John exited the color merchant's shop and stepped down the Place de Clichy, clasping a brown-paper-wrapped packet of paints and brushes. He hadn't been able to work all day, his nerves too wound-up, so he had walked the streets of Montmartre. He had passed by the Café Guerbois but Henri wasn't there. John had sat for hours admiring the nobles flocking to the Bistro du Royales. He had even considered drinking a glass of wine over lunch to settle his nerves.

John watched the sky change color as the sun set over the Paris rooftops. The contrast between the sharp, black lines of the buildings and the soft blues and oranges of the sky lightened his dark mood. A crow swooped over his head, its dark form appearing almost to be a piece of detached roof. The first wisps of night cloud started appearing. They thickened even as he stood watching the sunset. He wondered if a heavy rain was scheduled for that night. It had been unseasonably warm and the streets were foetid and dusty. He hoped for a clean start tomorrow morning.

Tomorrow.

He was to be the Queen's portraitist. At that thought, he felt his breath catch and his heart beat faster. This was his big opportunity. If he could produce a portrait of the Queen that was accepted into this year's exhibition at the Royalist Salon, his success was guaranteed. He smiled, picturing the accolades, adoring fans, generous commissions. He would be the greatest painter in France. He knew his mother would have been proud of him at this moment. He had so longed for that approval but she was dead and he would never be able to show her his success. He wished again that he and Henri were not at odds with each other.

Henri will share my happiness. Won't he?

John heaved a sigh. A raindrop hit his nose. Startled, he headed for home, intending to be indoors before the rain began in earnest. Indeed, it would be a heavy shower tonight if it was starting so early. The rain grew heavier and John turned up the collar of his jacket and lowered his head against the raindrops as he dashed through the wet streets. He hoped the rain augured well for tomorrow.

ಐ Φ ઙ

The imposing edifice of the Palace of Versailles loomed. He'd never seen this side of the palace. Its facade of windows, mullions, and cornices stretched to either side as far as he could see. John gaped up at the busts of Greek and Roman gods decorating the ruddy brick walls, his gaze skipping over the black Watcher spheres incongruously nestled among the carvings. The marble of the statuary was echoed by cream marble pillars on the corners of the building. Higher still, the glint of roofs and balconies edged with gold snared his eye. John smiled with pleasure. It was so very fine. John had been at the Palace before but this time it was different. This time he was here to paint the Queen of France. His feet crunched on the expansive gravel approach to the main doors of the palace. He had debated going around to the servants' entrance as he had in the past when arriving for sittings with members of the Court. This occasion seemed to demand a different protocol for admittance. He hefted his art case on to his shoulder and climbed the steps, his breathing a little faster than the exertion itself would warrant. Finally, he approached the liveried guards at the palace doors.

"Bonjour. I am here to paint Her Majesty," he said, flourishing his letter of commission. One of them squinted at the paper then replied,

"Wait here, m'sieur . . . Saylor. I will fetch the *Grand Chambrier*." The guard handed the letter back and turned with a whirring of gears. He walked into the palace, a clanking sound accompanying every other step.

An Augmented soldier, of course. Only the best and strongest guards for the royal palace. No doubt their mechanical prostheses are kept in optimal repair, unlike those poor veterans out on the streets.

The guard returned, accompanied by a bewigged man, tall and thin in a heavily embroidered silk tail coat and breeches. The Grand Chambrier was in full Court dress. John had encountered the man once or twice before, briefly. He didn't seem to remember the painter. John shifted in his brown wool suit, aware of the fraying cuffs and .the loose thread on one of the buttons.

"So. You are the portraitist, John Saylor? May I see your commission?" John nodded and handed him the letter. The man perused the page then examined John, his gaze traveling up and down John's unfashionable, slightly scruffy figure. He pursed his lips. "Come with me, m'sieur. You must be versed in at least the barest correct protocol for being in Her Majesty's presence before you are allowed into the Nobles' Salon."

John chose not to mention that he had been to the palace before and in the presence of nobility on many occasions. He followed the Grand Chambrier into the vestibule of the Palace and a forest of marble and bronze met his eyes. John was gripped by nerves as they walked, so intensely that he couldn't examine the magnificent decor of the interior. The air was still and cool. People bustled about, but they made little sound. They spoke to each other in hushed tones. No-one paid any attention to John although a few sketched a bow to the Grand Chambrier as they passed. The Grand Chambrier led him to a small antechamber and, turning, examined John again, his gaze lingering on the dust coating his shoes. John tried not to fidget under the man's inspection. The Grand Chambrier exhaled noisily.

"I suppose a painter cannot be expected to wear Court dress. *Alors*, there is nothing I can do about this. Your behavior I can manage, however. First and foremost, you are not to speak unless spoken to, do you understand?"

"Of course, m'sieur. May I apologize for my attire? Court dress is beyond my means."

The Grand Chambrier sniffed in response and continued his instruction. "When you enter Her Majesty's presence, you will lower your eyes and bow deeply." He proceeded to rattle off a list of prohibitions. John was sure he would forget most of them. His only hope was that no one would notice.

At last, the impromptu etiquette lesson was over. John

was led through multiple corridors that he had never seen. He had no idea how truly large the palace was. Some of the hallways were full of people while others stood empty. He wasn't sure if the Grand Chambrier was taking him by a circuitous route to the Queen's Chambers, but suspected that was the case. John would have no way of finding his way out and would have to rely on an usher.

ꕤ Φ ꕤ

At last they reached their destination, a set of tall white doors, decorated with gold, a brightly uniformed guard on either side of them. The floor was an ornate parquetry, glossy and smooth. Benches lined the corridor below the large paintings of war and royal ancestors. None of the people filling the benches wore the elaborate Court dress of the Grand Chambrier. John guessed that they must be common French people, probably here to petition the Queen with their problems. To his dismay, the Grand Chambrier stopped short of the doors and waved him to the wall. John glanced around but the benches were full.

"You will be summoned when the Queen is ready to receive you." Without waiting for a response, he stalked off, paying no attention to the crowd anxiously waiting for some sign that the time for their audience with the Queen was near.

John placed his art case carefully on the floor beneath him, brushes rattling inside as he did, then slumped against the wall. John saw one of the guards frowning at him so he straightened up. He tried hard not to fidget, remembering his mother's harsh admonishments about fidgeting. No-one spoke. They all appeared to be cowed into silence by the opulent surroundings. John surveyed the corridor, noting the lofty, arching marble ceiling. Each piece smoothly fit together, the muted colors of the stone varying slightly but creating a harmonious blend. Rich wallpaper in black and gold covered the wall. A creamy white statue towered above him, a goddess in flowing draperies, and another filled a niche at the end of the hallway, but John couldn't quite make out what it was. He spent some time examining the giant portraits of past nobility that hung on the walls. They were dark and somber, from another century. He hoped the Queen wanted something livelier.

Ushers showed the petitioners into the room at a painfully slow rate but then they seemed to leave quickly. Perhaps the Queen was feeling impatient today. He wondered how her impatience would affect the sitting. Would she move about? Refuse to hold a pose? Banish him after a few moments? He rubbed his forehead. He felt the beginnings of a headache. The room held too many people and not enough air. He pulled at his tight, high collar. His feet began to ache inside his hard patent leather shoes. The usher called out a name and an old man to John's right dragged himself to his feet. He shuffled forward to enter the salon. The instant he vacated his bench John quickly sat down, placing his art case on his knees. The smell of linseed oil wafting from the case calmed him a little and he closed his eyes. He breathed in slowly, trying to ease the nervous tightness in his chest.

A low boom from far off startled him and he jerked then opened his eyes, looking around. The chandelier above his head swayed, hundreds of prisms tinkling as they banged together. The men and women around him gasped and John saw dozens of wide-eyed faces and open mouths where before he'd seen nothing but glum looks and slumped bodies. The petitioners murmured questions to one another. John glanced at the guards, catching looks of alarm on their faces but the well-trained guards quickly suppressed their reaction and their impassive expressions returned.

What on Earth was that noise? Shouldn't they be doing something besides just standing there?

John waited, watching, but the guards didn't move from their posts. He peeked around the statue next to his bench but saw nothing unusual. The petitioners had quieted and an expectant hush filled the corridor.

The door to the Queen's Chambers clicked opened and a guard poked his head out of the gap. The three soldiers had a whispered conversation. John's eyes were glued to them, and he strained to catch their words. The guard reentered the Queen's Chambers without so much as glancing at the waiting petitioners. John groaned softly and shifted on the cold stone bench. He glanced around at the petitioners, taking in their tense, pinched expressions but none turned to leave.

John heard the tramping footsteps of a troop of soldiers before they came into view. Everyone shrunk back against the wall, women pulling their skirts against them as the brightly uniformed Palace Guard marched quickly by, clanking in rhythm. One of the soldiers stopped to talk quietly to one of the guards at the door. Finishing his quick conversation, he followed the rest of the troop. The whispers among the petitioners grew louder until at last, one man appeared to have been selected to be their spokesman. Hat clutched in his hand, he approached a guard.

"Pardon, m'sieur. What is happening? What was that noise?" The guard stared down his nose at the man.

"It is no concern of yours. Return to your seat, *citoyen.*"

With an unsatisfied twist of his mouth, the man walked back to the group of petitioners, huddled together now. Their faces looked unhappy and worried.

A few minutes later, two men in Court dress came striding through the corridor, whispering with heads together. They paid no attention to the crowd outside the Queen's Chambers but briefly stopped to talk with the guards, voices low. John struggled to hear their conversation but he was too far away. One of the petitioners must have been close enough to overhear. His face blanched. He slowly moved closer to the huddled group and peered over his shoulder at the guards before whispering to the petitioners. This time, John overheard a word.

Explosion.

His body tensed with fear. What could cause an explosion at the Palace? Perhaps a scientific experiment had gone awry in one of the laboratories? Silence reigned once more as the crowd stood, shocked by the news.

John spotted Scientists clad in their distinctive black outfits and uniformed soldiers marching through the hallway on their way to wherever the trouble was. The commotion died down after a time and the petitioners were again gradually allowed in to see the Queen.

ꝏ Φ ꝏ

John pulled out his pocket watch. He had been waiting for hours. He felt ill with nerves and hunger when one of the gilt doors opened and a liveried usher appeared.

"M'sieur Saylor, you may enter. Her Majesty is ready for you."

John stood, surreptitiously wiping his sweaty hands on his wool trousers. His suit was too hot for the stuffy Palace but he had felt obliged to wear it since it was his best. He followed the servant through an anteroom full of guards and then into the Nobles' Salon. It was a large room papered with apple green damask and decorated with elegant mahogany furniture. John quickly peeked up, spying a ceiling painted with gods cavorting in the heavens that he would have loved to stop and study, but the usher did not slow his pace. He led John through a crowd of noblewomen. They were all fashionably attired in dresses covered in ruffles and pleats, but their powdered, highly piled hair and white faces were reminiscent of a bygone era.

John trod on a noblewoman's train, not noticing in the press of people around him until she lurched against another woman with a scream. In an instant, hands steadied her and there was an outburst of noise as people gathered around her, solicitous and questioning. John tried to back away but the usher had his upper arm in a strong grip.

"M'sieur, please wait. We must be sure that Madame is well," he said. John was puzzled. She had just stumbled. How could she possibly be harmed? John sought out the woman's eye as she stood fanning herself, hand to her chest.

"I apologize, Madame, for treading on your train," he said with a half-bow. She glared at him but did not reply. John turned to look at the usher, his brow wrinkled.

"I'm sorry; did I commit a breach of protocol?" The usher shook his head and leaned closer.

"You could have killed her," he whispered. John glanced at the noblewoman then back to the usher.

"Killed her? How on Earth . . . "

"Her heart. A fall could stop her heart. She has one of those new-fangled hearts, you know. Self-winding." The usher puffed out his chest and smiled, seeming complacent in his displayed knowledge.

So there are Augmented people here among the courtiers too. They all look so human.

All must have been well. The usher gestured for them to move on. John scanned the crush of people. He searched for the Queen but had never seen her in person. Finally, the crowd parted and he found himself looking at a lovely mannequin, white-faced like a lady of fashion, in a sumptuous burgundy velvet gown. The automaton wheezed slightly and rotated to face him. Its mask moved slightly as words came out of its mouth.

"So you are the famous American portraitist, John Saylor, come to paint Us?"

With a start, John realized that this was no mannequin, but the old Queen of France herself. The Scientists had extended her life with what appeared to be extensive Augmentation. John had never seen a person Augmented so heavily. His throat suddenly dried out and to cover his revulsion, he sketched a quick bow, lowering his head so he didn't have to face the apparition approaching him. A whirring noise filled his ears as it—as she drew closer. John trembled.

"Your Majesty. I am honored to have this opportunity to paint you," he murmured. He rose from his bow with an awkward jerk and faced it.

Her, he had to remind himself in that instant. Not *it*. She was still a woman. The Queen of France. A woman with the power to have him imprisoned if she found him disrespectful.

The queen smiled ever so slightly, the enamel stilling her features into a vague melancholic expression. John studied her more closely, noting the exquisitely fashionable gown, an extravagant array of pleats, ruching, and ribbons. He turned his gaze to her face. It was more human up close, enameled, rather than a mask. He could see faint cracks in the enamel around her mouth and eyes. Then her eyes. They appeared to be blue glass, illuminated faintly from within. John had to suppress a shudder when he noticed their glow. Artificial eyes, their gaze drilling into him. Her intricate coiffure of blond ringlets and plaits was probably a wig, albeit a very expensive wig. She was indeed a fine example of fashion. The whirring was louder as she neared and appeared to be coming from her velvet-clad torso. Was there an electric-powered machine keeping her alive? Or was she merely an automaton? How much of the human was still left? He didn't know much of the science behind these half-human, half-machine creations. He was an artist and didn't care to know. Augmentation repulsed him. John even avoided the automated soldiers out on the streets, their stiff gait betraying the mechanical nature of their bodies. But now, here he was at Versailles, commissioned to paint this ersatz human staring back at him.

I am commissioned to make the Queen of France look regal and beautiful but if I paint it—her—as the mechanical horror that she is, I will be censured, possibly even imprisoned or hounded out of France for the insult done to its monarch.

"Are you making a proper study of Us so you can do Our beauty justice, painter?" the Queen demanded, breaking into John's reverie.

Flushing, John bowed his head and muttered, "I beg your pardon, Your Majesty. I did not mean to offend with my gaze. May I say that I am deeply honored to be your chosen portraitist, Your Majesty."

Without replying, she rotated and drifted towards a

chair.

She must be propelled by wheels., he thought with a shiver.

She turned back to face John and two stout ushers lowered her onto the chair. Her ladies-in-waiting fussed with the Queen's gown, smoothing it around her. Once she was settled, she beckoned to John.

"Come. We will sit here and visit with Our ladies. You may paint."

That said, she proceeded to utterly ignore him, chattering to the elegant ladies-in-waiting about inconsequential matters: fashion, horse races, theatre shows, and the like. A servant brought a table and low stool for him. John murmured his thanks, opened his art case, and set up the mini easel within. He began to sketch out the figure of the Queen, his hands shaking at first. But slowly, steadily, his breathing returned to normal as he fell into his work. He sketched the curve of her cheek, then her delicate nose and pointed chin. The face appearing under his pencil was a classical heart shape, the mouth a perfect rosebud. He no longer saw the monstrosity of the cyborg Queen, only lines and form to be captured on paper.

ꟷ Φ ꟷ

John was deep in thought, his hand moving fast across his sketch pad to capture the Queen's likeness as she shifted positions when he heard a rise in the noise level. He glanced up and saw two men in black entering the Nobles' Salon from a different door, carrying a large ornate metal key. Another man preceded them, clad in full Court dress: a tailcoat, knee-length breeches, lace dripping from the cuffs of his silk shirt, but all in black.

What a curious spectacle. Is he a Scientist or a Noble? I thought the Scientists eschewed Court dress.

An usher at the door declared, "Make way for the Royal Winder."

The man in black Court dress and the key-bearing Scientists stepped forward. All of the courtiers drew back, leaving a clear path from the door to the Queen. The Scientists slowly paraded towards the Queen, who sat waiting in her seat, head held high. John's hand slowed as he watched the Scientists bow deeply to the Queen then walk behind her.

The Royal Winder? Are they actually going to wind her up like some sort of clockwork doll?

He stopped sketching, his hand frozen above the paper. John tried not to stare at the Scientists bustling about behind the Queen. They seemed to place the key somewhere in her back. John didn't remember seeing any kind of keyhole in the Queen's back but perhaps he had only seen her from the front. She didn't react but sat motionless and silent. The courtiers were all quiet and attentive, faces turned toward their Queen.

The man in black Court dress did appear to be winding the key inserted into the Queen's back. John could hear the cranking of the key as it was turned. After a few moments, John saw the Royal Winder remove the key and hand it to his assistant. He looked around the room at the watching courtiers and declaimed, "The Winding is complete. *Vive la Reine*!"

In one voice, the gathered courtiers repeated the paean, "*Vive la Reine*!" and then they all politely clapped. Conversation resumed as the Royal Winder and his assistants departed through the same door they had entered. John sat for several long moments. He was so taken aback by this clockwork Queen that he simply didn't know what to do. The Queen resumed conversing with her ladies, seeming to be oblivious of his stillness. Apparently this interruption was a normal part of her day. After several deep breaths, he shook off his paralysis and continued drawing. He turned the page and sketched the Queen's face from a different angle since she had shifted her position yet again.

She does have a lovely face, even if it is heavily enameled. The Queen of France.

She was just as John had imagined: the quintessential Court beauty with that perfect complexion and fine aristocratic features. Her resemblance to a China doll was discomforting. Her ladies in waiting must perform some kind of magic during her toilette to maintain her looks after so many years.

He left after a few hours, somewhat satisfied with his sketches but still unnerved by the experience. The Queen took no notice of him when he finally left.

ည Φ ဗ

Adelaide stifled a yawn and fought off the urge to lay her head on her desk and nap. The laboratory was quiet and the afternoon sunlight beat against the heavy draperies, warming the room. The hush was broken by the scrape of metal on metal. Zoé sat at a workbench repairing a broken Watcher sphere. Adelaide watched as her assistant removed the smooth black glass lens to expose the inner mechanism. Corrosion speckled the wires and wheels. Zoé reached in and gently rotated a lever but it stuck.

"Madame le Professeur, could you come and take a look at this?" Zoé asked.

Adelaide met Zoé's eyes with a scowl. She had hoped

her assistant could make the repair to the machine without help. Zoé gestured to the disassembled Watcher, her expression helpless. A ruse to get out of work, Adelaide suspected. Sighing, Adelaide pushed herself to her feet and stomped over to the workbench.

"The lever is stuck. What do I do?"

Adelaide leaned over the girl, reaching into the Watcher's workings and wiggled the lever. She picked up a magnifying glass and examined the mechanism.

"Corrosion. The case must be leaking. It's very common with these machines. Do you see the speckling here? That will give you a clue to the problem. Clean off the corrosion and oil the moving parts. See if you can find where the case is leaking and seal that up." The girl nodded and tilted the sphere towards her. A glass plate slipped from its moorings and she tugged on it. It came loose in her hand. Zoé held it up.

"Madame le Professeur, what is this? There appears to be an image."

The women looked at the plate. A picture of a blurry street scene appeared burned into it. Adelaide shrugged.

"This is the image the Watcher captures. I can't tell what street that is, nor any detail about the people. How can that be useful for the Police Secrète?"

She shook her head and straightened. Adelaide arched her back, straining against her corset. She was stiff from sitting and longed for a walk in the rose gardens but her Automated Dauphin needed attention. Turning to the automaton lying on the table next to Zoé's workbench, Adelaide whisked the cover from the figure and smiled down at him.

"May I assist you, madame?" Adelaide glanced over her

shoulder. Zoé stood behind her, gazing down at the automaton, a strange unsmiling, yearning look on her face.

"No. You need to fix that infernal device or the captain of the Police Secrète will be here harassing me."

Zoé huffed and went back to her seat.

Such an impatient child. I suppose I was the same at her age but she needs to learn how to do the boring jobs before she can begin work on inventions.

The lab door banged open, hitting the wall. Adelaide started at the sound and turned to face the intruder. He was standing in the doorway, head thrown back, with that half-smile she remembered so well. Her stomach fluttered.

"Valmont. What are you doing in my laboratory?"

He strode through the doorway, not answering and not meeting her eyes, and surveyed the room. That damn smile still on his face. His examination seeming to be complete, he met her eyes. His smile deepened, showing the dimple on his right cheek. She tried to tamp down the rising excitement but his smile had always affected her. She noted that his black suit was well-tailored, fitting his broad shoulders perfectly.

"It's so good to see you after all this time, Adelaide."

Her hands shaking with emotion, she reached for the cover to conceal the automaton. She wasn't ready for anyone to see her secret project. She exchanged glances with Zoé, willing the girl to stay quiet.

Adelaide stepped away from the Automated Dauphin and walked around the tables and piles of equipment towards Valmont. He reached out and clasped her hands. A warm smile lit up his deep brown eyes. She gazed up at him. She'd forgotten how tall he was. He raised her hands to his lips and kissed them, lingering a little too long to be appropriate. Adelaide felt a warmth growing deep in her belly but with an attempt to control herself, disengaged her hands and stepped back.

"Why are you here, Valmont?"

"I'm here to inspect your laboratory, my dear. Didn't Monsieur Le Professor Piorry warn you that the Academy would send an inspector annually to be sure that your work met our standards?"

At Piorry's name, Adelaide felt her excitement at seeing Alain Valmont dissipate. Piorry certainly had not warned her about an inspection. Her transition from assistant to Royal Scientist Physician had been abrupt. The last she had seen her ex-mentor, he was being dragged off to prison by Palace guards after trying to kill her. She assumed he was still being held in the Bastille, although probably in one of the more luxurious rooms as befitted a high-ranking Scientist.

"And you're employed by the Academy now? I thought you were in Provence working on improvements to the weather machines?"

Valmont waved a hand in dismissal.

"Bah, listening to all those farmers complaining was boring and I didn't want to be stuck in the country. My wife complained continually about being so far from Paris."

Wife. So he married . . . I suppose his mother was responsible for him receiving the necessary authorization.

A flood of memories overwhelmed her: images of the two of them as students, laughing and strolling the streets together, intense discussions over coffee. All overlaid with longing and loss. He had tried to seduce her. Adelaide had first thought he was serious about her, wanted to marry her.

She would have given up science for him but she discovered that he had just wanted an affair. She was not well-bred enough for his family. Their breakup had been painful. And now he was married to someone else.

Adelaide brushed a strand of hair off her forehead, trying to ignore her shaking hand.

"Ah, yes. Well, shall we show you around? Zoé, show Inspector Valmont your work on the Watcher sphere."

Zoé shot a questioning look at Adelaide, clearly curious about Valmont, but Adelaide ignored it. Valmont leaned over the girl's shoulder to examine the sphere but straightened after a cursory look.

"Very nice. I'm sure the Police Secrète will be pleased that you are repairing their equipment but tell me, where are your innovations? You are the Royal Scientist Physician, Adelaide. The Academy expects a great deal from you. And what is the status of the Queen's health? When will she receive her Archimedean Heart?"

Rattled by his quick fire questioning, Adelaide hesitated. Her face burned and her eyes filled with tears. She turned her face away from him, unwilling to show him that she was distressed.

Damn him. He still knows how to disturb me.

Inhaling to calm her nerves, she blinked away her tears and faced him again.

"I am afraid the Queen's systems are too old. They will not function with the Archimedean Heart design. I informed the Academy months ago."

"Then how do you propose to replace Her Majesty's failing systems? Your last report on Her Majesty's health was quite dire. We assumed you must be working on an invention to solve the problems and repair her."

Adelaide opened her mouth to answer then closed it again. All of her spare time was spent on the Automated Dauphin but she wasn't ready to discuss that work. Zoé stood and broke the silence.

"Inspector Valmont, Madame le Professeur and I spend most of our time repairing these Watcher Spheres and taking care of the Augmented people here at the Palace. Madame Le Professeur is called to attend to Her Majesty's needs daily. We have very little time for experimental work."

Adelaide shot Zoé a grateful smile. Valmont crossed his arms and raised an eyebrow.

"And this is what I am to tell the Academy? You're too busy repairing machinery to find a way to save our Queen's life?"

Adelaide's eyes darted over to the covered automaton. Before she could respond, a blast shook the room, knocking the scientists off their feet. Zoé shrieked as she hit her arm hard against a table. A cabinet crashed to the floor, barely missing Adelaide and Valmont. Tools and equipment scattered out of the cabinet. Picking herself off the floor, Adelaide breathed the acrid smell of smoke.

"Fire! Something's on fire," she said, a panicky note in her voice. Scanning the room, she saw the smoke rising from a generator next to the Automated Dauphin. Her eyes widened and, pointing, she gasped out, "There!"

Valmont shakily got to his feet and moved away from the fire, towards the door. Adelaide scowled at his retreat and glanced around, looking for the fire blanket. Zoé had already reached it and was straining to bring it over to the smoking machine.

"Let me help you," Adelaide said, picking her way through the debris to the girl.

Mentally dismissing Valmont, she helped Zoé drag the

blanket to cover the generator, putting out the fire. She winced at how close the sparking, smoldering machine was to the Automated Dauphin but she dared not move him with Valmont around. The inspector stood in the doorway, watching. Adelaide stood upright and leveled a glare at him.

"I won't thank you for your assistance with the fire, Inspector Valmont. You will receive my report within the month. I bid you *adieu*." She turned her back on him and noticed Zoé grimacing and rubbing her arm. "Are you hurt, Zoé?"

The girl nodded, her eyes reddened. "My arm is very painful, madame."

"Let's take a look." Adelaide's tone was gentle, soothing. The girl had been hurt during a terrorist attack but had still put out the fire and protected the Automated Dauphin from harm. Adelaide felt a shift. Her assistant was not as immature as she had thought.

Five

The wrought iron chair dug into John's back as he slumped into it. An empty glass sat before him. He ran his hands across his head back and forth, tousling his usually tidy hair. Images of the Queen's sitting ran through his head, full of light and sound. That sound. The whirring noise that had been coming from somewhere in her torso—he could still hear it. Even here with the bustle of the evening crowd at the Bistro Du Royales, he could still hear it. He waved his hand at the waiter, who for once, came over immediately.

"Another," John slurred. He drank down the absinthe as soon as it arrived but the liquor couldn't still his thoughts. He continued to remember the strange, disturbing day at the Palace, the interminable wait, the mysterious explosion and then the Queen. Was she really just a mechanical doll? He shuddered. How could he continue with this commission when he felt nothing but revulsion for his subject? Those slightly glowing glass eyes rose up before him in his mind, their gaze seeming to pierce his soul to the quick. John felt bile rose in his throat.

What was the Queen thinking when she stared at him? Was she still a she? I have to create a beautiful painting of this china doll of a woman, this mechanical monster. How can I do that?

He didn't know and gestured for another drink.

"John?" A woman's voice interrupted his reverie. He squinted up and saw one of Desjardins' models, his current mistress, standing next to him. John struggled through the alcohol haze to remember her name. At the last moment, as she opened her mouth, seemingly ready to volunteer her name, it came to him.

"Ah. Isabelle. *Bon soir.*"

"Is there something wrong, John? I didn't expect to see you here, drinking the nectar of *La Fee Verte*. It is not like you, mon cher," she said. Her rough accent spoke to John of the uneducated masses, but her husky voice made him think of warm beds and wine. He shifted a little in his chair. She settled her lush figure into the seat opposite him. John gawked at her blearily then reached forward to grasp her hand across the table.

"Isabelle, I have to tell someone—I saw something awful. I cannot get it out of my head. What I thought once would be the pinnacle of beauty. It repels me. The artifice of the court—the automatons in power. It is wrong. It is vile. It is inhuman." His words poured out, lubricated by the absinthe. He let go of her hand and slumped down again in the tiny metal chair, knowing himself to be disheveled and reeking of alcohol. John saw Isabelle turn her head away from him a little, perhaps trying to avoid the smell but he continued his rant.

"I don't know what to do. I am supposed to paint her as a great beauty but all I see is the grotesquerie. Will they guillotine me if I paint an unflattering portrait of their mechanical queen?" A short, high laugh burst from him, hysterical.

He rubbed his stubbly face and scanned the patio for the waiter. Where was his damned drink? Spotting the waiter, John waved him over.

"Mechanical queen? What queen? What are you talking about?" Isabelle asked, a concerned frown on her face. John ordered his drink then smiled at Isabelle, a bitter twist to his mouth.

"The Queen. Her Majesty, Marie Thérèse, the Queen of France. I have the—ha! the honor of painting her portrait. God, how I wish I had never accepted the commission." His voice dropped to a mumble. "But how was I to know how vile, how monstrous she is?"

"Monstrous? What do you mean? The Queen is a beauty. Well, she was when she was younger, I suppose. What does she look like now?" she asked, her head cocked to one side.

"Isabelle, the Queen is nothing but a box of gears and an enameled mask. I knew they had Augmented her but I had never seen her, had no idea how . . . mechanical . . . she is."

"I've never seen her either. I don't think she has appeared in public for years. She is very old, I think. What do you mean Augmented? Do you mean like one of the soldiers with their mechanical arms and legs? Our Queen is this way? Is she no longer human?" Isabelle appeared to be faintly alarmed at the prospect. John said nothing. He sat back in his seat and closed his eyes. The waiter arrived with another glass of absinthe. John opened his eyes and drank, not looking at Isabelle.

"John? John, what do you mean? What does she look like?" John finally glanced up at Isabelle, feeling the stiffness of his face.

"She, she . . . I thought she was a mannequin at first. An

automated mannequin. She moves as if on wheels. Her face is enameled heavily. Her mouth barely moves. And her eyes. Oh God. They look like they are made of glass and . . . they glow." He shuddered at the memory. "And there is this, this whirring sound. From her chest. And then, oh God, the worst of it: they wound her up; they wound her with a giant key, like, like she was some sort of clockwork toy."

Isabelle drew back, face twisted in disgust at the image. In a low voice, she said,

"John, you must stop talking about this here, in public. You know the Police Secrète does not give second chances if they think you are—disloyal." Her eyes darted around the restaurant. John's mouth dropped open as he realized the danger he was in. The danger he had placed Isabelle in, just for having this conversation with him.

"I am sorry, I am so sorry, I didn't think," he babbled, reaching out to take her hand. She pulled it away and shook her head. He peered up at the balcony above the patio but didn't see a Watcher with its telltale blinking red light.

"Go home, John. You don't need to be out here in the state you are in. You could get into a great deal of trouble. Go home now."

Isabelle rose, bid him adieu and left hastily, looking around again as she left. He watched her turn the corner, then dragged himself to his feet. John swayed for a moment, and wagged his head, trying to clear it. He dropped money on the table, not bothering to count it, and staggered home.

ꕤ Φ ꕤ

Henri leaned against a window in his studio, watching the people go by in the street below. The glass was smudged, so he tried to clean it with his smock sleeve, forgetting that he had dragged his elbow through a pool of gravy earlier that day. He winced at the mess. The window was even worse so he gave up and moved to another window. Sycamore trees, their slender graceful branches reaching for the sky, obscured his view of the street down below. The leaves were changing to a deep red-orange color. They reminded him of Isabelle's favorite dress. It was a shade similar to the leaves and showed off her tawny skin to perfection.

Ah, Isabelle. He adored her lush curves, her pouting, smiling, laughing wide mouth and her soft, brown eyes. He stopped his reverie and frowned. Where the devil was she? She was late for the sitting. Ah, she was a delight but always, always tardy. Perhaps she had stayed late at the laundry where she worked. Or something else had grabbed her attention on the way and the time flew by. He knew that's what she'd tell him when she came flying through the door in a flurry of apologies and kisses. He smiled at that. Her kisses made up for a lot. And he would kiss her soon.

Sooner would be better.

Henri stayed at his smudged window watching the passersby until he heard the door click open. He turned to face it, a welcoming grin on his face. Isabelle slipped in through the doorway without a smile. She closed the door softly behind her and finally gazed up at Henri, her smile appearing at last.

"Isabelle, ma chère, you are late for me again. I sit and sit here waiting for you so that I can create magnificent art. What was it this time? Was it a stray puppy that needed you to help it find its way home?" he berated gently. She shook her head and said,

"*Pardon*, Henri. I am sorry to be late." He wondered at

her subdued manner and approached her with arms wide. Perhaps she thought he was angry. He enveloped her in his bear-like embrace.

"No matter, *chérie*," he growled in her ear. "You are here now. There is no need to be worried, *ma petite*. I am not angry with you." He drew back a little, took her face in his hands and kissed her wide, ripe mouth. She returned his kiss but without her usual ardor. She pulled back after a brief while then wrinkled her nose in repugnance.

"Oh, Henri, this place is disgusting. What is that wretched smell? And what do you have on your sleeve? Gravy? Faugh!" He bellowed a booming laugh in response and scanned his studio. Drifts of dusty clothing or possibly a drop cloth lay on the floor. Twisted, empty paint tubes littered the floor along with stale bread crusts, cheese rinds, and more than one empty wine bottle. Henri hadn't noticed the mess until Isabelle pointed it out. He shrugged.

"I can open a window if that would please your delicate nose, ma chère, but I am afraid the air outside may be a bit too chill for your tender, soon-to-be naked flesh. She grumbled as she flounced behind a torn, lacquered Japanese screen painted with cranes and cherry blossoms. She stepped back out a few moments later, clad only in a shabby cotton kimono. She shivered a little.

"Henri, it is freezing in here. Can't you light a fire?"

He shook his head sadly. "I have nothing left to burn, my frigid beauty. Perhaps my kisses could warm you up?" He approached her, trying to grab hold of her waist but she giggled and slapped his hand away.

"*Alors*, If I cannot have you, I must paint. We must begin before I lose the light. Come lay here on the divan, ma chère." She complied, dropping her kimono to the floor and laying down as instructed.

"Lift your arms back, ah, yes, there. Now turn your head away. Perfect." He reached forward to adjust the fall of her hair across her shoulders. He stepped back and nodded his approval. He moved behind his easel and picked up a palette and paints, brush tucked behind his ear as he prepared his colors. He began painting, not speaking, just looking up and down from the canvas to the nude woman sprawled across the divan. Her skin juxtaposed beautifully with the deep emerald fabric she lay upon.

Isabelle lay there silently for a while, as Henri painted her. Finally she broke the silence.

"I spoke to John Saylor today," she said from the divan. Henri grunted and continued to dab at his canvas, glancing at her, and then back down at the canvas. "He was drinking absinthe in the Bistro du Royales."

Henri glowered up at her from under bushy eyebrows.

"So that is why you were so very tardy today. A bit *luxe* for you, that place. Chin up a bit, *chérie*." She complied and went on talking, persisting with her train of thought.

"He seemed—distraught.

This provoked no response from Henri but she clearly intended to discuss the matter. She tried again. "Did you know that he is painting a portrait of the Queen?" At that, Henri stopped dabbing and stared at her.

"Huh. Why should I care what the Royalist salon adherents are doing? So he is churning out another society portrait, full of pretty, soulless images. He can take their commissions and leave the real painting to me."

She smiled a little mischievously at the vehemence she had provoked and went on.

"Ah, but he did not seem as triumphant as you would expect with such a commission. He said some . . . radical things about Her Majesty. Listen, Henri, John said that she was fully an automaton, that little if anything was left of the flesh-and-blood queen. When was the last time she appeared in public? Could he be right?"

He shook his head, frowning.

"The Queen is fully mechanical? I wonder who knows this. This news could change our strategy . . . "

Isabelle leaned forward, pose forgotten.

"Strategy? What do you mean?" Her normally husky voice was pitched higher. Henri smiled faintly at her.

"Nothing you need to concern yourself with, *chérie*. Pose, please. We have not got much longer since you were so tardy. I will lose my light." He gestured at her to resume the pose and attempted to go back to painting. She raised her eyebrows at him.

"Henri, have you become a man of mystery? All this talk of strategies. And who do you mean by we? Henri? Are you listening to me?" He gazed back at her in silence, deep in thought.

"*Cherie*, I do not want to endanger you. It would be best if you remained innocent of my concerns outside of the art world." Isabelle sat up, indignant, seeming to forget that she was naked.

"What? Innocence? You think me an innocent? That is ridiculous!"

Henri was nonplussed at the contrast between her vehemence and her naked body.

How do I ever get any painting done with her looking like that.

She glowered at him. Henri held up his hands in an attempt at placating her and walked over to her. He sat down next to her on the divan. She dragged her kimono off the floor and put it on quickly.

"Oh no, you don't, Henri, do not think you are going to seduce me into forgetting this. What is going on? Our Queen is some sort of automaton and now you have a strategy? And it is dangerous? And since when do you have concerns outside of the art world?" Henri grew still, his face solemn. He spoke in a low voice and she leaned closer to hear.

"Isabelle. A man came to see me. There is a movement to, ah, to replace the old King and Queen. There are rumors that they are no longer human. Now it seems that this is not just a rumor. You see, these people believe that the people of France deserve flesh-and-blood monarchs." He looked into her eyes. "And I agree with them."

Isabelle's eyebrows shot up, her eyes widened.

"Henri, that is sedition. Treason. You could be imprisoned for even talking like this." Henri nodded.

"I know. It is very dangerous but, Isabelle, this is a true and good cause. I promise you I will be careful. And you must promise me to say nothing of this to anyone." She nodded and said shakily,

"I promise." He held her close and she clung to him tightly.

ꙮ Φ ꙮ

The chattering of high spirited art students reached Henri before he crossed over the threshold of his former master's teaching studio. The bustling activity was just as it had been when he was a student. A model posed on a plinth in the center of the room, surrounded by students behind easels, all painting her just as Henri had once done. To one side of the room, tall windows offered a glimpse of the lush garden outside and let light stream in, highlighting the play of light and shadow on the model's deep brown skin. Henri admired her curves and wondered if he had painted her before. A wave of nostalgia struck him as he stood there enjoying the scene. He breathed in the unmistakable scent of Gleyre's studio—the smell of paint as well as the herbaceous, earthy scent of chrysanthemums. Gleyre adored chrysanthemums and filled the studio with bucketfuls of them from his garden when they were in season. It gave the studio the feeling of a festive funeral.

Henri's presence did not go unremarked and soon the chattering turned to buzzing whispers filling the room. The students all recognized the bear-like figure of Henri Desjardins, the man whose vibrant paintings matched his very public colorful life. They had no doubt all seen him striding through the streets of Montmartre, generally in the company of a beautiful model. He was a bit of a legend at the studio, he knew, one of Gleyre's students who had become wildly successful, albeit overseas rather than in his native France.

Gleyre must have heard the murmurs of excitement. He peered up from where he had been instructing a student. A smile lit up his pallid, wrinkled face when he met Henri's eyes across the room. He bustled over, arms outstretched.

"Henri, what a pleasant surprise! It is so good to see you! You're looking well." The men embraced. Henri gazed down at his old teacher. Gleyre was starting to show his age. Henri hadn't noticed how shrunken he had become.

"It's good to see you too, *cher Maître*," Henri replied. "You seem to be staying busy. Your atelier is full of students."

"Ah, yes, so many people are coming to Paris and they all want to be artists. I do what I can to teach them to be competent. But so few of them have that spark of creativity that you have. So few can really see what is in front of them." The old man shook his head, gazing around the room at his students. "Ah but I do have a most promising newcomer. He is from America. His name is Arthur Kendall. Perhaps your American friend John Saylor knows him?" Henri smiled. He knew Arthur was here and had come with the express purpose of speaking with him.

"Yes, John mentioned that he knew Monsieur Kendall."

"Huh, I suppose all these Americans in Paris know each other," replied Gleyre with a shrug.

"It does seem that way." Henri's eyes wandered the room looking for the subject of their discussion. Arthur was on the far side of the studio, looking intent on his work. Gleyre squinted at his students, trying to spot Arthur.

"He is here somewhere. I know I saw him today." Henri touched Gleyre's shoulder and pointed out Arthur. The old man grunted his response.

"I think that is him over there. I must go and give him John's regards. *Adieu, cher Maître*. Be well," Henri said. He sauntered over to Arthur, exchanging nods and smiles with the students he passed.

"Good day to you, Arthur!" Henri boomed as he reached his side. Arthur was deep in concentration and flinched when Henri spoke, dropping his paint brush to the floor. He stooped to pick up the brush. Dust was stuck in the paint. Arthur frowned at it.

"Oh, I beg your pardon. I didn't mean to startle you," Henri said. Arthur smiled a small, tight smile.

"Monsieur Desjardins. Have you come to share your artistic wisdom with us?" Henri felt a little deflated at Arthur's formality and was that sarcasm? Ah, this was not the way to start the conversation he wanted to have with Arthur.

"Please, call me Henri. I feel that as you are a friend of John then you must be a friend of mine. Come, let me take you for a coffee." Henri felt in his pocket for some coins, hoping he'd have enough to treat Arthur. Arthur's face softened and he smiled with more warmth.

"That would be delightful. I think I am finished with the structure of this piece."

Henri examined Arthur's sketched-out painting of the voluptuous model. He had made her seem more angular than in real life but somehow more alive. Henri nodded his approval.

"She is so alive, she could almost step off the canvas."

Arthur beamed at Henri's appraisal. He removed his painting smock, revealing an elegant grey and black checked suit. They headed towards the entrance of the studio.

"I am stealing your student away for a coffee," Henri told Gleyre as they departed.

ജ Φ ഗ

Arthur and Henri paced the steep, narrow streets of Montmartre in a companionable silence. Finally, Henri broke the silence.

"I truly admire how alive, how real and human your paintings are. Your people are neither dolls nor daubs of color. Where does your inspiration come from?"

"Where but the source of all life," Arthur's face was calm, placid. "My inspiration comes from He who created us."

Henri was nonplussed. Arthur was religious? He believed in a god? How very unusual. Henri gazed up at the blue sky, framed by trees and high buildings, then down at Arthur.

"So then you are a Naturalist."

Arthur's forehead creased in confusion.

"A Naturalist? I am not sure I know what you mean by that. You are not saying I'm some ungodly heathen, are you?" Henri chuckled.

"No, not at all. I mean one who believes that people should align themselves with Nature, not machines . . . " Henri stopped as an Augmented policeman clanked by on the pavement, limping a little. He must have just one mechanical leg, Henri thought. He tried to keep his face impassive. It was not healthy to sneer at the Augmented ones; they tended to take offence. Arthur examined Henri's face, then watched the passing policeman. People stepped out of his way, their eyes lowered.

"We do not have all these machines in America. I hardly know what to make of them. Are they all veterans of war that were grievously wounded then repaired by your Scientists?" Henri nodded, his eyes following the policeman's progress along the road.

"Some of them. Although you may see pensioned-off veterans with useless mechanical arms or legs. The army abandons them when they are no longer needed, then their prosthetics wear out and break."

Arthur tsked at that. "Some of them. Only some of them needed their limbs to be replaced? Are you saying that there are Frenchmen who volunteer to have perfectly good limbs taken off to be replaced with Augmented ones?" His face contorted in horror at Henri's nod of assent. "But that is terrible. Unnatural."

"Unnatural. Exactly. This is what our love of science has wrought." Henri scanned the street around them before saying in a hushed tone, "And it is worse than that. I have heard that our Queen, our beloved Marie-Thérèse has been transformed into an almost entirely mechanical creation. And worse, our King has been ill for many years and no-one has seen him since I was a boy. Who knows if he is still alive?" His face sagged with melancholy.

"Henri, this sickens me to hear. Why do the French people not speak out against this atrocity? They should rise up against these aberrations." Henri put a stilling hand on Arthur's arm and shushed him.

"Not so loud, mon ami. There are those who watch and listen all around us and this talk is seditious." Arthur glanced around, eyes wide. The street was bustling with innocent-looking shoppers carrying net bags full of food.

"But why do you endure this state of affairs? Other countries have thrown off the shackles of tyranny."

Henri shrugged. They began walking again, avoiding other people. "It is because we are so well-fed. France is exceedingly prosperous. Our harvests are always abundant because our weather is always perfect. It's because of the Scientists and their weather control machines. We are ruled by rational men, these Scientists. Arthur, we French are well-treated, like pampered animals in a king's menagerie. What do people care for naturalism and freedom when their bellies are full thanks to the machines?"

"I think then that the French may be well-fed, but they have lost their souls," Arthur said.

Henri nodded. "Yes, I fear it is true. That is why I must support the Naturalist movement. Only they can bring back France's soul."

Arthur cocked his head at that. "Ah, so that is what you

mean when you asked if I was a Naturalist. You were not just speaking of a school of painting."

"No. It is a movement to put the true king of France on the throne. He will subdue these Scientists and all their. . . inventions." He said the word as if it tasted bad in his mouth. "They do good, I grant you that, but they control Nature too much for my tastes."

Now it was Arthur's turn to hush Henri. He said in an undertone, "You are talking about a rebellion. Replacing your monarchs with another."

Henri stopped to face Arthur, a defiant tilt to his chin. The street around them was empty.

"Arthur, France must be freed from these cyborg royals. The spirit of France will wither and die otherwise."

"This is a dangerous thing you are attempting, especially since you say there is constant surveillance." He gestured at the buildings around them but there were no Watchers visible. "And how can artists such as ourselves be of any assistance?" Arthur appeared troubled, grave of face. Henri assessed what he knew of Arthur. How far could he be trusted? He seemed sympathetic to the cause. He took a breath to steady himself and faced Arthur.

"It is difficult and dangerous, *oui*, but we must do this, we must free France from the tyranny of the machines. We need assistance from everyone, yes, even artists such as ourselves. We too can watch and report what we see. I must ask you, Arthur—are you willing to help free France?"

"Well, I must admit, I had no idea that I would be involved in a social upheaval when I came to France. I had no idea how deeply the machines had infiltrated daily life. Henri, I must ask you to wait for my decision. This is too important for me to decide on my own. I must pray about this." At that, Henri was reminded again of how different he and Arthur were.

They continued their stroll to the Cafe Guerbois and passed into the bustle and noise of the coffeehouse. Their conversation turned to art and good coffee. The men did not bring up religion again. Henri could only wait and hope that Arthur's god would be supportive and that Arthur would join the Naturalists.

ꝏ Φ ꝏ

Adelaide ambled through the winding path around one of the many fountains in the gardens of Versailles. She had strayed into the public gardens, entering through a private entrance from the garden reserved for members of the Court. She knew few of the courtiers would think to look for her in the public areas so her privacy was assured. She wouldn't be disturbed in her reveries Walking helped her think, so she walked and walked through the paths for hours. She needed to find a way to smooth out the power fluctuations for the power supply in her newest automaton. She worried about the Queen as well. Her electric modulator was failing again and Adelaide wasn't sure she could fix it this time. The bonds between machine and human were failing as the Queen's remaining human parts grew too old to function anymore, even with mechanical assistance.

She turned onto a secluded pathway winding among high hedges, breathing the spicy scent of the laurels. A man clad in a sober wool suit was leaning over a woman in a bright gown lounging against a tree. He was smiling down at her and as Adelaide watched, he leaned down and kissed her deeply. The woman's arms wound around his neck and she returned his kiss.

Kissing in public! They are obviously commoners.

Despite her condemnation, Adelaide stood rooted to the spot, unable to tear her eyes from the ardent couple. Her breath grew shorter.

No-one's ever kissed me like that. Valmont only hinted at such desire. I wonder what it would be like. But that will never happen. I would lose my position if I were to . . . indulge.

Adelaide licked her suddenly dry lips and rubbed her arms, disturbed by the tingling warmth across her skin. Pulling her gaze away from the pair, she forced herself to leave.

She pushed her hair off her forehead as she strolled, staring without seeing the people strolling through the gardens alongside her. A burst of laughter close by startled her out of her daydreams and she turned in the direction of the sound. A trio of women sat under a tree, pushing each other and giggling. They were common laborers from the looks of their faded, plain dresses. A burly, dark man stood in front of the group, an easel set up next to him. A painter. He too was laughing and waving a brush at the merrymakers. Adelaide drew a little closer, wondering what was amusing them so much. She heard the man telling the women a bawdy joke which made them all scream with laughter. All of a sudden, the women fell silent, looking over his shoulder at Adelaide. He turned and saw Adelaide standing there, a flush across her round cheeks as she stood there awkwardly in her sober black gown.

"I beg your pardon, Madame. Did I offend you with my naughty jokes?"

"I, uh. No. That is, um . . ."

The painter smiled at her hesitancy and sketched a mock bow in her direction. The women behind him tittered.

"I beg you to please forgive my indelicate conversation,

dear Madame. I am Henri Desjardins, a humble painter, and am most honored to make your acquaintance, Madame. . . " he fished for her name and smiling shyly, she said,

"Adelaide."

"Adelaide. What a charming name, perfect for such a charming individual such as yourself. And are you alone, sweet Adelaide or are you accompanied by your fierce tiger of a husband?"

"No, no, that is—I am not married." At that, the painter's smile took a mischievous twist and he said,

"Then indeed I am most fortunate this day to make your acquaintance for I too am unmarried. Pay no attention to those women; they are merely artists' models. It matters not at all that I have seen them completely and utterly without clothing. It was purely for art, you understand." Adelaide blushed again.

"Do forgive my disruption of your painting session, Monsieur Desjardins. I must be away. My work—I must return to my work." The man guffawed and grabbed her hand.

"No, no, sweet Adelaide, don't leave me yet when I have just discovered your charming self. Work? Bah! What work could be more important than lounging here in the sunshine and having a glass of wine with me?" She tried to retrieve her hand but he held it fast. He tugged gently and she moved a little closer. "Will you partake in a bit of wine, dear Adelaide?" A slight smile appeared on her face unbidden but she shook her head.

"No, I must not. Drink will fog my mind. I must be clear minded or I will make mistakes. I cannot afford any mistakes at this juncture." The painter tipped his head, eyebrow raised.

"Do tell, what is this ever so important work of yours

that you must stay completely sober to do?"

ꕥ Φ ꕥ

He stopped talking and scrutinized her attire. Plain, serviceable black, but made from expensive materials and tailored perfectly. A silver badge pinned to her bodice bearing a fleur de lis crossed with the Greek letter Phi. It was suddenly clear to him.

"You're a Scientist," he muttered, his smile fading from his face. He let her hand go and stepped back. She belonged to the Scientist class, those responsible for creating all the Augmented soldiers and policemen clanking around Paris, for the ominous Watcher spheres perched on rooftops and balconies, and for the Weather Machines that made it rain at night but not during the day. These Scientists had caused the movement away from real humans, away from Naturalism. She had seemed so human, so real. He wondered if she, too, were Augmented.

"Yes, that is correct, I am a Scientist. More specifically, I am the Royal Scientist Physician." Henri nodded slowly, his lip curling.

"I see. And what are you doing out here with us commoners? Slumming? Looking for subjects to experiment on and study?" the woman drew back at his vehemence.

"Merely taking the air. I bid you good day, sir." With that, she pivoted and marched away, her boots crunching the gravel. Henri watched her go, feeling disappointed and somehow angry that she was one of Them. One of Henri's models piped up,

"Henri, whatever were you doing flirting with a *Scientist*? As if she would take you seriously. You would never get anywhere with her."

"And what would Isabelle say?" asked another.

"Isabelle is not my wife," Henri snapped in response. "I am done here. You can go home. Here is your fee and your train fare." He pulled coins out of his pocket and handed some to each of the women as they stood, stretching and shaking out their skirts. He started packing up his brushes and paints. The models ambled off, calling their goodbyes but Henri didn't look up. He had enjoyed teasing Adelaide when he thought she was a shy widow. But a Scientist? He shuddered. He abhorred everything she worked for. His musings were interrupted when a shadow fell across him and he glanced up. It was the man who had stolen into his apartment and spoken to him of revolution.

"Jean-Luc. What brings you to the Pleasure Gardens of Versailles? I would think being this close to the Palace would be a bit daring." Jean-Luc stared blankly at him. "The Palace. Where the monarchs live?" Jean-Luc shook his head.

"It matters not. The people in the Palace do not know who I am. I am safer here than near the Bastille where the Police Secrète is based. Desjardins, do you know who that was you were speaking to? The woman in black."

"Yes, her name is Adelaide. She says she is the Royal Scientist Physician but she seemed too young to have such an important position. I thought she was probably someone's assistant." Henri shrugged. Jean-Luc's face twisted with anger.

"Fool, she works directly with the King and Queen. She is their personal physician. She is the person keeping them alive. What did she say to you?"

"Nothing much. I was flirting with her. I had thought her widowed and in need of a little fun, if you know what I mean." Henri winked knowingly at Jean-Luc who pursed his lips.

He was quiet for a moment then Jean-Luc said,

"If you were to . . . become intimate . . . with her, you could learn important information about what goes on inside the Palace. We need to know more so that our attempts to make change are more successful."

"Intimate? With her? Did you see how rigidly she held herself? I would wager that one has never known a man between her thighs."

"Good, she will be easier for you to seduce, since she is inexperienced. It is vital that we know how many guards are inside the Palace, where they are posted and when and where they move. She may let these details slip if she is relaxed. You can get us this information and aid the cause."

Henri groaned and nodded his assent.

"Very well. Isabelle is going to kill me. Ah yes. Jean-Luc, I have something I need to tell you." He surveyed the crowded gardens "Not here. We should meet somewhere else."

"I will contact you with a time and place"

Jean-Luc disappeared without another word. Henri finished packing his supplies and sauntered off through the gardens to the train station. He supposed he'd be returning to Versailles again soon to complete his assignment. Seducing a virgin Scientist. He shuddered. He really hoped she wasn't Augmented. He didn't think he'd be able to perform if she were.

℘ Φ ℘

An usher escorted John into the Nobles' Salon for another sitting with the Queen. The young courtier was there; the one John had seen faint in the garden when he was on the way to the duchesse de Fronsac's last sitting. The girl sat next to the Queen, fanning herself. The room was warm and stuffy, crowded with dozens of courtiers. but the girl seemed apart from them. The Queen spoke to the girl who never looked up but sat still, staring at her hands, nodding. Her face was too pale, John noticed, but not from cosmetics. He wondered if she was ill. Consumption took the young as often as the old. He found himself saddened at the idea of this lovely young girl dying prematurely from that terrible disease.

Shaking off his morbid thoughts, John approached the Queen, smiling and bowing. She returned his bow with a nod and returned to chatting with her ladies-in-waiting. The servants brought over his easel and set it up, putting the canvas in place. John studied his painting and then the Queen. Inwardly, he groaned. The gown he had painstakingly depicted on the canvas was not the one the Queen currently wore. He decided to work on the background instead but found himself sketching her, the young one seated next to the Queen. What was her name? He strained to hear the ladies talking and heard a name.

Marie-Ange.

She was a much more attractive subject than the aging mannequin of a Queen. He caught the girl's eye and smiled. A tinge of pink stained her cheeks and she dropped her eyes again, waving her fan a little faster.

"Have you just arrived at Court, *mademoiselle*?" he asked from behind his easel. She darted a quick look at the Queen before replying,

"*Oui*, Monsieur Saylor. I am new to the honor of serving Her Majesty here at Court." Her formal words vied with her sudden wide smile and she continued, "Life here at Versailles is so exciting! I had no idea how big it was and Paris! So full of life and excitement! And the Palace is much grander than I had imagined." John smiled at her youthful exuberance. How did she know his name? Did the ladies of the court talk about him?

"You are from the country?"

"*Oui*, m'sieur, from Aix-en-Provence. It is very quiet there."

"Ah, but very beautiful. Both in scenery and those who inhabit it." Marie-Ange blushed at his flirtatious comment, obviously not used to the way men spoke to her at Court. He smiled at her, charmed by her innocence.

"Are you enjoying painting our Queen?" she asked. John stopped smiling, his face froze into a polite mask. He studied the painting . . . he'd almost thought the word *ordeal*, he struggled so with depicting the Augmented Queen and paused before he responding.

"Of course, mademoiselle. Her Majesty is a formidable subject."

The girl's face fell and then she blurted out,

"Forgive my stupid question, m'sieur. I know nothing of what it is to be an artist."

"Please do not worry yourself. There is nothing to forgive, truly." He gazed at her, smiling warmly. "There is really no mystery in art. We simply do as our Muse bids us."

"A Muse? How perfectly delightful! And who pray tell is your Muse, m'sieur?"

"A person of singular beauty, an ideal figure, inspires my art."

Their conversation was interrupted by the appearance of the woman who seemed to be the Court doctor. She had entered without the usual fanfare but all the Court ladies sank into deep curtsies as she passed. John was surprised at the courtesy.

"Bonjour, Madame Le Professeur," many courtiers

murmured. The new arrival glanced around and smiled before approaching the Queen. John noticed that she did not curtsy to the Queen.

"How are you feeling this morning, Madame?" she asked. The Queen shook her head, lifted her hand slowly and grasped the woman's hand. The Scientist Physician nodded and gestured to the waiting ushers. They raised the Queen from her chair and the Queen left, arm-in-arm with the woman. John was puzzled and irritated.

"I suppose the sitting is over," he said to himself and began packing his supplies.

Marie-Ange leaned down and said in a soft voice, "Her Majesty is not feeling well today. I fear she may be in need of another treatment. Madame Le Professeur works hard to keep her well."

"She is quite advanced in her years, is she not?" asked John. Marie-Ange's face was grave.

"Indeed. She celebrated her 102nd birthday this year."

John blinked. "I had no idea. 102 years. Really? How is that remotely possible?"

"Our scientists are gifted in extending life through automation. Do you know it was the Queen's father who first created the mechanical prosthesis?"

"Astonishing. I had no idea."

"We keep our technology secret. Outside of France, no-one knows what our Scientists have created." Marie-Ange peeked at him from under her eyelashes, her smile tilted. John's heart thumped and he felt a flush rise in response to her proximity. He rose from his stool with a jerk and bowed to the noblewoman.

"I must be going now that my subject has departed." He picked up his art case and hurried out, disturbed by his visceral reaction to the young girl's flirtation. He thought of his mother insisting on purity and felt a pang of guilt for his momentary weakness. She would have disapproved of a flirtation with a young innocent noblewoman, knowing that it would not end honorably. He resisted the urge to look back as he left the Nobles' Salon.

ꝏ Φ ꝏ

Electric lights blazed in Adelaide's laboratory as she leaned over her battered desk, writing in a thick book. Zoé labored nearby, calling out numbers. The young woman had her head almost fully inside the chest of the Automated Dauphin. Adelaide huffed out a breath and pushed wisps of hair off her face.

"Zoé, there is still error here. Can you adjust that hydraulic valve in the left shoulder?"

"*Oui*, Madame Le Professeur, but I fear the connections will not take more pressure."

The pair continued tinkering until Adelaide straightened and slammed the notebook shut. She rubbed her aching neck and stretched as far as her corset would let her. Wretched thing. Men's clothing was so much more practical but Her Majesty would have been horrified if Adelaide dispensed with her corset and petticoats and gown in favor of a simple shirt and trousers.

"I can do nothing more today. I have no more time. I must give some attention to the Queen. Her electric modulator is fluctuating out of range again. Zoé, I am not sure how much longer I can keep her going. Her systems are failing faster than I can Augment them." She felt her stomach clench at the thought of the ailing ancient monarch. Zoé pulled her head out of the automaton's innards and stared at Adelaide.

"I beg your pardon, Madame Le Professeur, but why is the Queen so essential? His Majesty rules us. Well, with the assistance of Presidente Le Scientist."

Adelaide scrutinized Zoé's innocent face, assessing whether to trust her. Despite her arrogance, the girl showed no signs of Naturalist leanings. The girl gazed back at her, her young face sweet and guileless. Exhaling softly, Adelaide decided it was too risky to unburden herself, although she desperately felt the need for a confidante here at Court.

"The Queen is just as important as His Majesty to the French people. They all love her and wish her well, even if she does not control the government like Presidente Le Scientist. This automaton will—assist—Their Majesties."

Zoé tilted her head at Adelaide, an eyebrow raised in question.

"I don't understand. How will the automaton assist them? Will it walk for them? Carry them?" Her face looked uncertain. "I've never seen His Majesty. Does he require carrying?"

Adelaide snorted.

"Not exactly." She couldn't say more without betraying state secrets. The King did not move or speak anymore. The Queen had become his voice. No-one saw the old King except for his personal servants, the Queen, and Adelaide herself. "Have you begun the work on his speech processors yet?"

Zoé shook her head, still frowning in confusion.

"Not yet. Madame Le Professeur, how will this automaton aid the King and Queen? Will he speak for them?"

Adelaide waved a hand in dismissal. She would not divulge the true purpose of her Automated Dauphin until he was fully operational.

"Never mind his future role. Please do your work. It is

imperative that he be completed without delay."

Zoé nodded, unsmiling. She moved closer to the automaton and gazed down at it. "I see. We have much work to do before it functions correctly. I'll continue working here while you are with Her Majesty." She picked up a tool and began calibrating it.

"*Merci*, Zoé. I will return as soon as possible." She left the room in a rustle of dark taffeta.

Six

The sun glared overhead, illuminating the fashionable as they strolled through the Bois de Boulogne. John sat on a bench, watching them pass. He recognized a few of his clients but they didn't acknowledge him. He pulled out his sketch pad, more to have something to do rather than from a desire to draw. His eye found no interesting subjects. Only painted approximations of beauty, like china dolls. Their unpainted attendants were worse: blemished, with greasy, unkempt hair, and ill-fitting clothes. He had hoped to surround himself with beauty but all the people he saw were imperfect, marred in some way.

He winced and turned away, spotting Henri across a green expanse of lawn. His brother stood behind a canvas, painting a group of people lounging by the water.

What does he see in those common people?

Intrigued, John got up and wandered closer, trying to stay out of Henri's line of vision. He wasn't sure if Henri was still angry with him over their last meeting. John felt ashamed again. He dearly wanted to make matters right with Henri but didn't know how to go about it.

Henri was painting a scene of what appeared to be a group of whores and their men, the assembly all lounging and having a meal *al fresco*. John's lip curled in disgust at the frowsy women laughing and talking and eating all at once. The men were somehow even worse, slovenly and crass. He saw one reach out and squeeze his companion's bottom as she leaned across to get more wine. She screamed with laughter and playfully pushed his hand away. Henri stood painting the scene, smiling at the antics of his models but not speaking. He was painting fast. They were liable to leave as soon as the wine was gone so he needed to get the scene onto his canvas. John marveled at his quick, sure brushstrokes. He didn't enjoy Henri's subject matter but he had to admit that the man was a master of his technique. The scene came to life in bright colors and broad strokes. John walked closer and Henri glanced over at him. The older man grinned.

"John! I wondered when you would appear again. Are you over your fit of pique? Hah! I see you could not stay away. You needed to watch a true master create yet another spectacular piece of art? I think perhaps you wanted to see why I paint my unlovely subjects. Look, it is all right there in front of me. Can you see the character, the life right there in front of me? I paint people, John, not pretty things."

John merely nodded, not rising to the bait. He was relieved that Henri was still speaking to him, even if his brother was continuing his lecture.

"I must admit to being impressed by your composition and color but I still see no purpose in painting—that." He gestured at the group. One of the women caressed her man's hair. She grabbed his lapels and kissed him hard. John turned away and goggled at Henri, disgust written on his face. Henri laughed his booming laugh and waved his brush towards the scene in front of him.

"Mon frère, this is life. Pure, unadulterated life. It matters not if her hair is mussed or his suit is stained. The imperfections simply highlight their natural beauty to me; it shows the life in them." Henri gestured towards one of the women. "Look at the way the light catches her cheek just there as she laughs. That, mon frère, is worth painting."

John shook his head, still not understanding. All he saw was unattractive, uncouth people lounging on the grass.

"I am sorry, my friend. I just do not see it," he admitted.

He took his leave of Henri and wandered through the curving paths of the rose garden. More elegantly dressed Parisians passed him but their attempts at beauty failed to thrill him. The excess of pleats and frills on the trailing gowns of the women struck him as being ridiculous and overdone. The enameled white faces struck him as being more mannequin than human. He searched in vain for a lovely, unpainted face and simply dressed dark hair. A woman both pure and lovely, just as his mother had urged him to paint.

A woman like Mother, before she grew ill.

John felt a pang of guilt. He had been unsympathetic to his mother once she lost her looks to the illness. He hoped she never knew how it revolted him. She had been so lovely when she was younger. Even his childish sketches of her showed an exquisite woman.

John realized with a start that he was searching the gardens for a beauty reminiscent of the young courtier he had encountered at Versailles.

That girl, Marie-Ange. I should paint her.

He strode through the garden, spirits restored.

ꙮ Φ ꙮ

Adelaide gazed thoughtfully at the automaton, its mechanical frame contrasting oddly with the finely finished wood table he was laying on. The light glinted off his strong profile, a portrait of the King in metal. Adelaide intended the likeness to be a deliberate reminder of his function, that of a monarch. She leaned closer to the automaton's face and stroked it tenderly. Her voice was low, her lips inches from the metal face beneath her.

"What will happen to us? Our King and Queen have no issue, no surviving human Dauphin to succeed the King when he dies. And despite my efforts, the King has not much time left."

The automaton was silent and Adelaide didn't know if she'd ever be able to give him a voice. Without the King and Queen, the duc d'Orléans would return to France and steal the crown. Adelaide had heard rumors that he had sworn to depose the Presidente Le Scientist and undo all the good that science had created in France.

Her scrutiny traced his still face, searching his empty glass eyes for a response.

"Our only hope is you, my Automated Dauphin. You will be able to usher in true democracy to France."

She bit her lip and stood up straight, pushing the hair off her forehead. Her laboratory was warm and stuffy but she dared not open a door or pull back the heavy brocade curtains to open a window. It was too risky. Someone might glimpse her creation before it was complete. She was counting on the element of surprise to win over some of the opposition to her scheme to bring true democracy to France.

She sighed. If he was ever complete.

Adelaide placed a gentle hand on the prone figure of the

automaton. She wound his clockwork heart and closed the little brass chest plate.

"We need you. You will be France's democratic leader. When you are functional, I have designed you to be capable of receiving all the voices of the French people and making decisions for the greater good, not just the rich and powerful. You will be an impartial, immortal leader, free from the vagaries of emotion."

She waited, but no glimmer of light appeared in his blue glass eyes. His lustrous brass heart was beating but the energy wasn't transferring to the control cylinder. She exhaled a heavy, deep sigh.

"But if I don't get you functioning in time, all my work will be for naught. The duc d'Orléans will return and sweep away all of the reform we Scientists have brought to France in the past eighty years. I simply cannot allow that to happen. You, my Automated Dauphin must be fully operational soon."

She opened up his chest again and with her electric light examined the convoluted innards of her Automated Dauphin. She saw it almost immediately; a crucial connection was missing. She searched for the glass and brass piece but it was gone. Puzzled, she pushed aside some clutter on her workbench, but it wasn't there. She called out.

"Zoé? Have you seen the main power regulator? Zoé? Where the devil is she?" She exhaled heavily and surveyed the room for her errant assistant. Adelaide walked to the door of her workroom and poked her head out. Zoé was lounging against the wall, a flirtatious smile played across her lips. An usher leaned over her. They were talking in low voices. Zoé glanced up and her face grew ashen when her eyes met Adelaide's.

"Zoé! You are not employed in this laboratory to pursue

your love life. Come in here immediately! I require your assistance." Adelaide glared at the usher who sketched a quick bow before wandering off with a backwards smile at Zoé. The two Scientists walked back into the laboratory in silence. Adelaide slammed the door and barked, "The main power regulator for the automaton is missing. Where is it?"

Zoé cringed a little before replying, "I beg your pardon, Madame Le Professeur. Please forgive me for neglecting my duties. It will never happen again, I promise, Madame Le Professeur."

Adelaide huffed with impatience. "Never mind that. Where is that blasted regulator? The automaton cannot function without it."

"Forgive me, Madame Le Professeur. I, ah, I removed it for repair. It, um, I think it shorted out or, um, possibly clogged. I have not been able to make it function. I think it may be too lightweight for the electric current passing through it."

Adelaide swore under her breath. If that was the case, she'd have to redesign the wretched piece. She rubbed her forehead, pushing back her hair again. Then it occurred to her that electric components didn't clog.

What was the girl talking about? Did the Academy assign someone to me who doesn't understand automatons?

"Zoé, whatever do you mean? The regulator can't clog. Let me see it." Zoé startled a little, looking confused.

"Clogged, did I say it clogged? I mean, no, it cannot have clogged, electric regulators don't function that way."

Adelaide huffed again and said, "I know that, which is why I asked you to clarify. What a fimble famble! So it shorted out? Let me see the wretched thing."

Zoé glanced around and shrugged, her face reddening.

"Forgive me, Madame Le Professor. I can't remember where I placed it. I was attempting to install the regulator earlier today but noticed that the bulb appeared to be cloudy. So I assumed it must have shorted."

"Huh. That does sound like it overloaded. Where could you have put it? I must see it in order to determine the extent of the damage. If the overload was minor, we may be able to add more resistance to that piece."

She rummaged around the workbench. It was a mess of gears, wires, half-assembled components and tools. "I cannot believe you lost it. Zoé, this is a crucial piece and it took me weeks to assemble. I will need to order the machinists to make new parts. *Zut!* This will set the project back months." She was pushing things aside more quickly now, parts rattling and crashing against one another. She picked up a chunk of metal and threw it hard against the table. "Where IS it?!"

She kicked the table leg and stalked over to the huge mahogany cabinet. She yanked open the doors and glared over her shoulder at Zoé who stood watching her, a look of trepidation on her face.

"Zoé! I need light! Why haven't we installed lights inside this monstrosity of a cabinet? I can't see a thing in here." Zoé scurried over with a portable electric light and held it aloft behind her shoulder. After a few moments of cursing and shuffling pieces about, Adelaide cried,

"Aha! Here it is!" She turned around and held the component up to show Zoé. She nodded weakly. Adelaide examined the piece, a puzzled look on her face. "Zoé, I do not see any cloudiness. What made you think it had overloaded?"

Zoé stammered a bit and said, "I thought, um, I saw, er, that is, perhaps the light was bad?"

Adelaide glowered at her, an eyebrow lifted in disbelief. "The light? Do you mean these new-fangled, incredibly brilliant electric lights? They were not bright enough for you to be able to distinguish whether the bulb was clouded?"

Zoé dropped her head. "Forgive me, Madame Le Professeur."

Adelaide snorted and walked over to the automaton. She inserted the power regulator back into the chest of the Automated Dauphin and restarted the heart. The machine began humming and the glass eyes began to glow faintly. Adelaide grinned. Then with a spark and a hiss, the humming ceased. Her grin faded along with the fading light from the automaton's eyes.

"Blast. Now what is wrong? We need to get to work. We need to get him functioning as soon as we can. We don't have much time left. If the King . . . "

Zoé bowed slightly. "Of course, Madame Le Professeur. I will get started immediately." Adelaide grimaced. Perhaps if she supervised the girl more closely, she wouldn't make mistakes.

Zoé positioned a magnifier light over the automaton's chest, bringing into sharp relief its inner workings. The Scientists stood side by side, searching for the shorted piece under the bright light.

ᘓ Φ ᘐ

John followed an usher through the maze of hallways in the Palace towards the Nobles' Salon. They turned onto yet another hallway and their feet clattered onto wood, contrasting with the marble flooring from the previous hallway. John's gaze dropped and he saw a herringbone pattern of parquetry, glossy, fine wood pieced together perfectly. He hadn't noticed any of this on his last two visits to paint the Queen. John noted the exquisite painted wood panels on the wall and ceiling and paused, wanting to view them more closely.

"Please, could you wait one moment?" he asked the servant who turned, frowning ever so slightly. "I wish to examine these panels. I remember the way to Her Majesty's rooms. You may go on without me."

"Of course, Monsieur Saylor."

Relieved of his duty, the usher bowed and strode off towards the Queen's chambers. John became quickly engrossed in examining the panels. The panels were intricately hand-carved, then painted bright colors. They appeared to be heraldic, consisting of shields divided into geometrical shapes. He wondered what they signified. He drew closer, the fine wood of the frames almost begging to be touched. He reached out and lightly traced one of the geometrical patterns, enjoying the feeling of the carved wood under his fingertips.

He heard the clatter of high-heeled slippers and quickly pulled his hand back from the wall. He turned and saw Marie-Ange approaching. She was alone. His heart rate picked up a little at the sight of her. She smiled her open broad smile as she came closer and recognized him. She was a true beauty, her cheeks paler even than the enameled ladies around her. How astonishing her pallor seemed to him, coming from the streets of Montmartre where almost everyone had some color to their skin. Her family down in Provence must have been isolated from the influx of immigrants from the French African colonies.

"Bonjour, Monsieur Saylor," she said. "The usher returned to the Nobles' Salon without you. I thought you might be lost." Her ivory cheeks had a touch of red today and her eyes were bright. John felt his throat thicken at the vision of her vital beauty and he swallowed hard before responding with a bow.

"Mademoiselle de Laincel. You look radiant today." He found himself unable to say more and broke off, staring at her lovely young face. She was once again in a plain white gown, her thick dark hair unpowdered and pulled back into its simple chignon. At his compliment, her cheeks grew pinker still and she dropped her gaze.

"M'sieur, you are as charming as any of Her Majesty's courtiers."

"Ah no, please do not think I am giving you empty compliments, mademoiselle. Your beauty. Your beauty stuns me."

Marie-Ange lifted a hand to her chest and shook her head slightly, not looking up. "I am but an unsophisticated country girl. I am nothing compared to the lovely ladies of the court."

John stepped forward and raised a hand as if to touch her shoulder, but dropped it to his side again. "No. Your beauty is real and true. Your beauty owes nothing to cosmetics or fancy gowns. How I wish . . . " He stopped himself, wary of overstepping his bounds.

She finally met his eyes and asked, "What . . . what do you wish?"

John contemplated her longingly before responding. "I wish the circumstances were different."

Marie-Ange nodded, head drooping. "Yes. I understand. I am so young. So inexperienced. A man of the world such as yourself—"

John interrupted her with a gentle hand on her arm. "Marie-Ange, your youth is an asset, not a liability. It is your station to which I refer."

Marie-Ange hesitated then burst out, "My station! All my life I have been constrained by my position. I was never allowed to mingle with anyone outside my family because they were too common. Ah, but, M'sieur Saylor, I disliked it so. I never felt that it was right. I do not feel superior just because of who I was born. My blood runs as red as anyone not of noble blood. It is so unfair. Why should I not do as I please, speak to whom I please, be with whom I please?"

John shook his head at her vehemence. "None of us can do as we please. If I could, I would . . . " He stopped himself, knowing he stood on dangerous ground. She gazed up at him, her dark eyes wide.

"What would you do?" Her voice was a little husky. The sound of it, low and rough, reminded him of the sensual Isabelle and he shivered, blood suffusing his face. This time, instead of leaving her abruptly, he moved a little closer to her. She was petite and had to tip her head back to look into his eyes. She licked her lips nervously and his eyes shifted to watch her mouth.

"I would . . . ah, I would paint you. And I would paint you with nothing on so I could see all of your smooth, luminous skin." He saw her tremble and their eyes locked. He was desperate to touch her, to feel if her skin was as soft as it looked.

"Yes? And then?"

He smiled, feeling wicked, and leaned down towards her, his mouth close to hers. He could feel her warm breath on his mouth and paused, looking deeply into her eyes.

"*Mon ange*," he whispered. Footsteps clattered behind them and the couple sprang apart.

"Marie-Ange! Marie-Ange! Where have you disappeared to? I have been waiting an age for you!" A slender foppish courtier approached them, high heels tapping on the parquetry. He was frowning ferociously and glared at John. "What ARE you doing with this—*pouah*—this painter? And alone! Dearest child, this is positively scandalous! What would Her Majesty think if I told her?" Marie-Ange blushed, her face a mask of misery and embarrassment.

"Please do not say anything, Mercoeur. I was just showing John, I mean Monsieur Saylor, the, um, the . . . "

"Panels," John interjected. "Mademoiselle de Laincel was showing me these fine panels and explaining their significance." Mercoeur glared at John.

"Did I address you, painter?" His words were injected with venom.

"Mercoeur! That is discourteous!" Marie-Ange said. Mercoeur turned to Marie-Ange, his face adopting an ingratiating look as he took her hand and placed it on top of his raised forearm.

"My dear girl, one cannot be courteous to low-born people like painters. It would simply encourage them to rise above their station and that would not do. Why the fellow might get ideas about you and take liberties. They have the morals of a house cat, you know. Always seducing their models and the like."

At this John burst in with, "That is a lie! I am not an amoral seducer. My models are perfectly safe with me."

Mercoeur laughed at him. "Oh ho, the worm turns! You expect me to believe that you do nothing when a woman is lying naked in front of you? Truly? Well, then perhaps instead you prefer the Athenian approach?" He winked at John who turned away in disgust.

Marie-Ange appeared confused by this exchange, and gawked from one man to the other trying to understand.

Mercoeur ignored her inquiring look. “Come, Marie-Ange. Let us walk in the gardens. The private gardens reserved for nobles such as ourselves.”

John gazed at Marie-Ange, her hand held firmly in place on top of Mercoeur's. The courtier smirked and whisked Marie-Ange away. John, fists gripped at his side, watched them go until they turned out of sight. He continued on to the Nobles' Salon, fuming with impotent rage. He would be late for his sitting with the Queen but he didn't care.

ꙋ Φ ꙋ

John left the Queen's chambers after a grueling two hours trying to paint her. He had found himself scraping off more paint than he put on the canvas so had made no progress at all. He simply couldn't find the beauty in her, a rarity for him. But then he'd never tried to paint an automaton before. After several hours in her presence, he was convinced that little remained of the human Queen. His lack of progress could also have been attributed to his desire to paint the beautiful Marie-Ange. He couldn't focus on the Queen. He had drifted into daydreams about removing the young woman's hand from that odious Mercoeur's arm and taking her away from here. It was a ridiculous dream. What did he have to offer a young French noblewoman, accustomed to costly gowns and magnificent *chateaux*? His little house in the disreputable artists' quarters of Montmartre? He quietly laughed at the notion. Still, he couldn't get her out of his mind. She was simply the most beautiful woman he'd ever seen. It was no wonder that Mercoeur sniffed around her skirts. John entered the same hallway where he had almost kissed Marie-Ange earlier. He couldn't believe Mercoeur had discovered them in that deserted corridor. It was almost as if the courtier had sensed that Marie-Ange was with another man and searched for her.

John again examined the heraldic panels on the wall as he passed them, wondering if one of them symbolized the de Laincel family. Marie-Ange was from an ancient noble line, so chances were her heraldry was represented here. John felt insignificant in this hallway of noble French families, an American with little history and even less prestige. Disliking the feeling all those heraldic panels gave him, he hurried on his way, heading down to the tradesmen's entrance. He passed servants and courtiers in the chequered hallway but didn't see Marie-Ange. His heart sank a little. He had hoped to spot her once again before leaving that day.

Disappointed, he headed through the servants' hall to the tradesmen's entrance. The kitchens were busy, servants bustling to and fro preparing a feast for the nobles upstairs. His stomach growled. He had forgotten to eat before heading to Versailles that morning and now it was mid-afternoon. Jeanne was sitting peeling potatoes. She glanced up and waved, a smile on her sweet face.

"Bonjour, John! Which of our lovely court ladies are you painting now?" she asked.

"I have the honor of painting Her Majesty," he said, with the barest hint of a smile. Her mouth dropped open and she gasped.

"Truly? I have never seen her! Is she as beautiful as they say?" John paused, not quite knowing how to respond.

"I hope to accurately portray her. You will have to wait and see."

Jeanne frowned, seeming to be unsatisfied at his evasion. John continued, "Can I beg a bite to eat from you? I have not eaten all day."

"Of course, you want a little bit to carry with you? Let me get you some bread and cheese." She rose from the table and scurried around, quickly slicing bread and smearing some soft cheese on it. "There you are! We cannot have a court painter dying of hunger, *non*?"

John thanked her. He cocked his head to one side.

"Jeanne, why is it that I've never sketched you? Such a lovely face as yours should be immortalized."

Jeanne giggled and waved a hand in dismissal.

"Silly! Why would anyone want a drawing of me? Besides you're much too busy painting all those noblewomen so they can make their husbands happy."

"One day, sweet Jeanne, I will come and draw you. You can give it to your mother."

ꕥ Φ ꕥ

John left, wandering into the vegetable gardens, nibbling on his snack, and from there into the rose garden. The riot of colors filled his vision and he stopped short. Reaching down, he gently caressed a crimson petal and stood mentally composing a painting for a few moments. John would have loved to stay and paint the flowers but the *Grand Chambrier* had not given him leave to do so. He walked along slowly, trying to fix the scene in his mind so that he could paint it when he returned to his studio. Looking up at the sky, he saw that it was later in the day than he had realized. By the time he reached the Versailles train station, took the train back to Paris and then walked to his studio, it would be dark.

He sighed. So much for painting something truly beautiful that day.

He had hoped to cleanse his mind of images of the

Queen by painting those roses. The circuitous path he took around the flowers delayed his exit from the garden. He glimpsed a flash of white between the linden trees on the periphery of the garden and stood still. Was it Marie-Ange? Very few young girls lived at Court, so he didn't see many women in simple white gowns here. He waited, straining to see who it was. Finally, she appeared in full view. John's heart raced as he recognized Marie-Ange. She was in a group of court ladies, trailing behind them and looking about as if searching for someone. Her eyes found John's and she paused, darting a look at the ladies preceding her. They didn't seem to notice that she had stopped. When they were several meters ahead of her, she stepped behind a large hornbeam hedge, its tall narrow shape forming a passageway with a matching hedge. The ladies wouldn't be able to see her if they turned around. John began strolling towards the hedge, searching the gardens for anyone paying attention to him or Marie-Ange. His heart was pounding. The noblewomen all seemed intent on chatting and strolling. A pair turned in his direction and he froze. They stopped and began an animated discussion about the brilliant red roses in front of them. John glanced back towards Marie-Ange. She was no longer visible. He crept towards the spot she had been standing. The noblewomen continued their conversation. As he drew closer to where Marie-Ange had been, he saw that she had preceded him into a narrow passageway of hedges. He peeked in. Her white dress was gleaming in the dark between the bushes. She was alone. He surveyed the area quickly then hurried down the passageway towards her, his heart racing. Her smile seemed to light up the gloom cast by the tall hedges.

"John," she said quietly. "I am so glad I spotted you before you left. You left your art case." She handed him the case as he reached her. He placed it on the ground, took both her hands in his and smiled tenderly down at her. She had called him John. He trembled as he held her cold little hands.

"Marie-Ange. I barely dared to hope that I would see you again today. Thank you for bringing me my case." Her smile deepened and she squeezed his hands.

"I must apologize for that cad Mercoeur. He was so rude to you. He seems to think we have reached some sort of agreement but my father assures me that I am unpromised."

"He is of your class, my dear. You must know that I cannot aspire to your level, even if you are not to marry another."

She shook her head, dislodging a lock of her thick brunette hair. It fell against her cheek. He released one of her hands and reached up, smoothing back the hair behind her ear. His hand lingered there for a moment, then gently touched her cheek. She inhaled sharply and he felt her cheek grow hot under his hand.

"Please, John. Do not talk to me of class and position. I am so weary of it. This Court life does not suit me. I wish I could run away but I am honor-bound to serve the Queen." Her eyes silently pleaded with him.

"Do you wish to go home, back to Aix-en-Provence?"

"No, not there. If I were released from my service to the Queen, I could . . . " she stopped and drew back. He took his hand away from her cheek. She dropped her eyes from his, frowning.

"Marie-Ange, this is impossible, you know." Her eyes flew back up to his face.

"Impossible? Please do not say that. You are the first taste of life I have had. I want more." She moved closer to him, placing a hand on his chest. His heart thudded at her touch. "Please," she whispered. Her eyes fluttered closed. John could not resist the invitation and bent his head down to hers. Slowly, gently, he covered her mouth with his. His kiss was tender and quick but it seared him. She was delicious. He pulled back.

"I should not have done that," he murmured. "But I want to do it again." She opened her eyes. They were misty and love-struck. She nodded, seeming unable to say more. After a moment she said again,

"Please."

Regaining control, he shook his head, drawing back.

"I would not be a man of honor if I continued to take advantage of you, *mon ange*. This is wrong, illicit. It is not worthy of a lady such as yourself." Marie-Ange bit her lip at the rebuke and pulled back her hand.

"I apologize for being so forward, m'sieur," she said with a sob in her voice, her eyes filling with tears.

"No, please do not apologize; it wasn't your fault, Marie-Ange. It was my fault. I took advantage of your youth. I deeply apologize. Please forgive me. How I wish our courtship was not impossible, but it is. I must go before we are seen and your reputation ruined." He bowed to her and turned away.

"John?"

He turned back. Marie-Ange stood there holding his art case out to him. John took the case and hurried away, leaving her standing there between the dark hedges. He didn't see the tears flowing down her cheeks but guessed they were there. It wasn't his place to stay and comfort her.

Seven

The small cafe near *L'École des Beaux-Arts* bustled with harried art students bolting their lunch. Henri sat nursing his cup of coffee, earning disdainful looks from the pallid waiter. The disdain was understandable. Henri had been sitting there for over two hours, waiting for his contact from the Underground. He drummed his fingers on the little metal table and let his gaze drift across the room again. Where was that confounded man? He had told Henri that any time he wanted to meet, he was to come here at noon and wait.

I hate waiting.

He would rather be strolling up and down the streets of Montmartre, watching the people of Paris go by. He might even spot a new face he had to paint. Sometimes, a scene would strike him and he would pull out his sketch pad to capture it. So many types of people lived in the *arrondissement*, from all the French colonies in Africa and the West Indies. Then there were the African-American émigrés. As he had told Arthur, they received much better treatment here in France than they did in America. Despite the white monarchs and their fawning nobles, most Parisians welcomed the people of color who flocked to Paris to enjoy her culture and way of life.

Where was Jean-Luc?

Henri would have left already but he needed to tell someone in the Underground what he had learned. It was vitally important, this knowledge he had received from Isabelle. Surely the natural king would return to France if he heard that the monarchs had been Augmented until they were no longer human. The Scientists needed to be brought down to the level of the people. Once the duc d'Orléans was King, he would get rid of the privilege afforded to the Scientist class, and take away the power they had usurped.

A rattling, wheezing steam bus went by. Its noise caused all conversation to cease. The Duc would get rid of all this machinery. Paris would be peaceful without the Augmented Police Secrète and the machines huffing up and down the streets. Henri wondered what it would be like when rain fell sporadically, without warning like it did in the old days before the weather control machines. He thought he would prefer it. Having something natural like rainfall on a schedule seemed wrong to him.

He scrutinized the bright blue sky.

How he tired of that constant sunlight. He wished for some cloud cover. It would change the light in his paintings to have clouds covering the sun. He wanted to explore that.

The students began to dissipate. It was past their lunch hour and still Henri waited. He considered ordering another cup of coffee but could only afford the one. Perhaps Jean-Luc would buy him a meal. Anything to stop that waiter from glaring at him.

Without warning, Jean-Luc appeared at his side. Henri

got a better look at him in the daylight. Scrawny and ashen. I guess the Underground doesn't pay well, Henri thought.

"Monsieur. You are well, I am hoping?" the man asked. Henri nodded and gestured towards the chair opposite. The man shook his head. "I will not sit, we must walk."

Henri sighed. So much for a free lunch. He climbed to his feet and threw his last remaining coins on the table. They left the cafe. Henri pointedly ignored the sneering waiter as he walked past. The crowds were out, trying to enjoy the last pleasant days before the chill of winter set in and the streets were slick with ice. The Scientists could control rainfall but they couldn't control the coming of winter. Henri lost himself in watching the people walk by, composing pictures in his head. He was startled when Jean-Luc spoke.

"Well? Have you information to share? I would have you speak quietly, even out here on these streets." Henri wondered at his strange diction. He certainly didn't sound French.

Unable to suppress his curiosity, Henri asked, "Your accent is most unusual. Where do you hail from, mon ami?" The man's face became more pinched.

"I am of French stock." Henri waited but no more was forthcoming. Jean-Luc was also watching the crowds, albeit a little more anxiously. Without warning, he grabbed Henri's arm and attempted to pull the bigger man into a doorway. Amused, Henri allowed Jean-Luc to tug him along and they entered a small shop. Henri examined the little room. It was a china shop, selling all manner of delicate tea sets, knickknacks and figurines of the Queen dressed as a shepherdess.

"What—" Henri began but Jean-Luc was peering out of the small window set in the door, not paying any attention to Henri. Henri heard a woman clear her throat and turned to see the shopkeeper approaching, a confused look on her face. Jean-Luc and Henri were not her usual clientele.

"How may I be of assistance, *messieurs*?" she asked. Henri, thinking fast, met her eyes and stretched his mouth into a wide smile.

"Ah, Madame, how nice it is to see you. And how are you feeling today? You are looking very well." The woman's face grew even more confused and she hesitated, obviously attempting to figure out who he was.

"Monsieur. I am well. And—how are you?" Henri was relieved. She had decided to play along. Henri had never seen her before but perhaps his charm would buy them time while Jean-Luc continued to survey the street outside. He was attempting to think of something else to say when Jean-Luc jerked at his sleeve and muttered, "We must be going now."

Henri bid the shopkeeper *adieu* and the men departed. Once outside, with the shop door shut firmly behind them, Henri asked, "*Mon cher* Jean-Luc, what was the meaning of our little foray into a china shop, of all places?" The other man's face was sullen, or was that fear writ on his face?

"Did you not hear the policemen with the clanking as they walked by? I do not wish for them to see me. The streets are becoming too dangerous for me to be here. Let us find a place that is not so public." Henri nodded and led him to the alley behind Edouard's wine shop. After surveying the little alley intently, Jean-Luc said,

"Please, you are to tell me the knowledge you have learned."

Henri took a deep breath and tried to organize his thoughts.

"As you know, my friend John is also a painter. He has

a commission to paint the Queen. He came back from Versailles with a strange tale. He says that there is little of the human left in her. The Queen has been Augmented so much that she is practically an automaton."

Jean-Luc shook his head and whistled softly. "An automaton. We had heard that she was Augmented. She would have to be. Did you know she is over one hundred years old?"

Henri raised his eyebrows and asked, "How is that possible? Her portraits show a lovely youthful woman."

"Those portraits are many years old now. They have been reproduced over and over to fool the French people into thinking they are current likenesses. But now you say your friend is painting a new portrait?"

"Yes, but he is struggling. He is so repulsed by her that he can hardly work. He is afraid of what will happen if he is unable to produce a pleasing portrait." Jean-Luc was silent for a moment before asking,

"Is he sympathetic to our cause?" Henri shrugged.

"He may become so. I think he is still too infatuated with the glamor of the Court to turn against it at present."

"It would be most advantageous for us to have someone with access to the Court. You will keep me with the knowledge from your friend John? And you see if you can convince him to join us?"

"Yes, of course."

"And the Scientist? Have you ingratiated yourself yet? She has direct knowledge of the King and Queen and may know about the guards' movements." Henri squirmed. He had tried to forget about that little assignment.

"Not yet."

Jean-Luc grimaced at him and Henri shrugged. "I will go back to Versailles and try to find her," he promised.

Without saying goodbye, Jean-Luc slunk around the corner and was gone. Henri grimaced. He was not fond of the subterfuge. It was uncomfortable and worrisome. But he supposed it was a necessity if he wanted to see a human monarch ruling over France. He gazed longingly at the back door of Edouard's shop. A nice bottle of brandy would settle his nerves but he was out of coin and out of credit with Edouard. He made his way home, musing on the strange turns his life had taken. Just a few weeks ago, Henri worried about little more than having enough brandy. Now he was engaged in revolution. How would it all end?

Ah, perhaps I'll have more money after the revolution and can buy all the brandy I want.

ᘓ Φ ᘕ

Henri wandered through the Gardens of Versailles. Crowds of Parisians filled the winding pathways, taking advantage of the waning warmth of the autumnal sun.

These gardens are ridiculously immense. I will never be able to find that woman.

He pulled out his pocket watch and checked the time. He had been looking in the public section of the gardens for the woman Scientist for an hour, hoping to catch her on one of her walks. Henri searched but saw no-one clad in that severe, simple black gown that she wore. His fellow Parisians were dressed in their colorful Sunday best, out to enjoy themselves.

Why did I accept this ludicrous assignment? Seduce a Scientist and get her to divulge state secrets? I'm an artist, not a spy.

He supposed he could seduce just about any living, breathing woman, but was this one even alive? He was still worried that he'd get her undressed and find mechanical workings instead of womanly parts. He shuddered at the thought but the problem was moot if he couldn't find her. He tried to recall where he had been painting when she had wandered by. Ah, yes, one of the groves. He made his way to the group of artfully arranged trees. They seemed to be planted to provide a dark, secluded spot for forbidden rendezvous. Henri chuckled.

Ah, those naughty kings of the last century. They knew how to enjoy themselves. Before the Scientists took over and made my France boring and sterile.

He wasn't paying attention to his footing and tripped on a protruding tree root. He landed on the ground with a thump, with his ankle twisted below him. Henri bellowed in pain, his ankle seeming to be on fire. A cold sweat came over him from the pain. He shivered and cursed, trying to stand but his ankle wouldn't support his weight. He fell back onto the ground, groaning. How could he be so stupid as to not watch where he put his feet? He scanned the grounds for help but saw no-one. The gardens were crowded but this isolated spot was empty, ignored. He cursed again, trying to decide out what to do but the pain in his ankle made it hard to think. He sat there for long moments, hoping someone would come close enough to see him there. After what felt like hours, he saw a pair of young holidaymakers heading to the grove, probably hoping for some time alone. They were bound to be disappointed since Henri was in their chosen secluded spot.

"*Pardon*! Please? Can you be of assistance," he called out to them, trying to rise. "I appear to have injured myself."

Looking concerned, the couple hurried to his side and began asking questions. The woman took a look at his swelling ankle and shook her head.

"Ah, *m'sieur*, your ankle is most definitely in need of a doctor. Look at how swollen it is. There could be broken bones. Perhaps we can ask someone in the Palace for help?" The man concurred and hurried off. Henri sat with his head in his hands, fighting back tears.

What if it's broken? How will I work with a broken ankle? What if it doesn't heal properly and I can't walk?

His worries were interrupted by the man's return. He was accompanied by a woman in black and with a start Henri realized that it was her, Adelaide. He remembered then that she was a Scientist-Doctor. He hoped she knew how to treat human patients as well as mechanical ones.

"Well, m'sieur, let us see what you have done to yourself," she said, focusing on his injured ankle. He sat in the shadows and she didn't appear to recognize him.

"Are you to be my angel of mercy, sweet Adelaide?" he purred. She glanced up at him in surprise and recognition dawned on her face.

"Monsieur Desjardins! I am sorry; I did not recognize you at first." He shrugged, a crooked smile on his face.

"No matter. I am pleased to see that you are here to assist me with my injury. I know I am in good hands." He intended for his tone, warm and husky, to imply more than medical assistance. She blushed. Henri watched with delight as color flooded her cheeks. He no longer felt the pain as strongly. Her hair wisped around her face and with the blush, she looked like she had just stepped out of bed.

Perhaps this won't be so onerous an assignment.

“Can you stand at all? I need to take you back to my laboratory to treat this,” she said. At that, Henri froze in horror. Her laboratory? What was she going to do to his ankle? Would she replace his flesh with some mechanical apparatus?

“No, no, I don’t need your help. I’ll just go home and rest it.” He lurched to his feet but his ankle was still too painful to stand on and he stood there on one foot, feeling slightly ridiculous.

“Nonsense, you cannot walk on that ankle. How are you planning on getting home? Will you hop all the way back to Paris? Stay there, I will be right back with help.” With that, she strode out of the grove to summon some of the Palace guards.

ฆ Φ ଔ

Despite his protests, within a few moments the guards were carrying Henri towards the Palace, Adelaide trotting along beside him. He was helpless and more than a little frightened. They headed into the Palace and despite his fright and pain, he looked around. He'd never been inside this edifice that had been erected in a more decadent time. Its opulence stunned him. He had had no idea quite how magnificent it was. Distracted by the decor, he barely registered when the little entourage stopped in front of a set of ornate doors. Adelaide fished out a key from somewhere in her voluminous skirts and unlocked the doors. The guards carried him into a darkened room, full of strange shapes, metal glinting in the half-light. He was here. In one of the Scientists’ mysterious workrooms. He wondered what would become of him. Would she lop off his foot and replace it with one of those unreliable mechanical prosthetics? Would he then be unable to go out in the rain at night?

Adelaide directed the Guards set him down on a long table.

"Come now, m'sieur, lie back so that I can examine your ankle more thoroughly."

Henri shook his head. He felt a little more in control sitting up. It would be easier to get off the table and away from her if he needed to.

"No, I don't need to lie down, I would rather sit. And really, Madame, I don't need your help, I'll be fine. Please let me go home."

She tsked at his reluctance and dismissed the guards. "Very well, sit up if you must. Your ankle could be badly injured, m'sieur. I must examine it."

He watched the Scientist move around the laboratory, switching on lights, lights brighter than he had ever seen before. They shone steadily and with a strange blue-white light, completely unlike the lantern or candlelight he was used to. He squinted against the brightness.

"What are those lights?" he asked. "They're so bright." Adelaide smiled, almost proudly, he thought.

"They are electric-powered. They are the lights of the future. Soon, all of Paris will be lit by electric street lamps. They are much brighter than gas lamps, as you can see, and so will better deter crime."

"Ah, but where will mystery and romance go when those lights chase it away?" he responded.

Adelaide shook her head in response, although he spotted a smile tilting the corners of her mouth.

She gently pulled off Henri's worn shoe and shabby sock. He looked down and saw that his ankle was swollen and starting to bruise. It was so swollen, it almost looked as if someone had stuck half a peach on to his ankle. She tsked at the injury and gingerly pressed on the inflamed flesh. He gasped quietly from the sudden stab of pain and saw her frown.

How bad is it? Am I going to be crippled?

She straightened up and walked across the room to a large cabinet, He was too worried about the upcoming treatment to look around the room but glimpsed glinting metal and machinery in his peripheral vision. What he could see did not reassure him as to his fate. She returned to his side, bearing a short, brass baton. It hummed slightly when she flicked a switch on its handle. He stared at it as if it would bite him. Adelaide finally seemed to realize that her patient's silence was born of fear. He locked eyes with her and she smiled reassuringly, her brown eyes warm.

"There is no need for you to worry, Monsieur Desjardins. This will not hurt." He was unconvinced and shook his head.

"What—what are you going to do to me with that thing?" he stammered then loudly burst out, "I don't want to be Augmented!" Adelaide laughed and patted his knee.

"I am going to remove the swelling from your ankle, not give you a new one!"

He grimaced, feeling stupid and cowardly.

So much for Henri, the smooth and charming Lothario. I'm sure she's very impressed with my manly fortitude and bravery now.

He allowed her to press the small device against his ankle. The vibrations were cool and soothing. The throbbing in his ankle started to ease. He watched her face. She was intent on her task. Her hair was even more bedraggled than before and she pushed it back with an impatient hand. Henri noticed that her mouth was wide and lush. He tried not to think about how it would feel on his. He shifted a little and she glanced up, a concerned frown on her face.

"Does this hurt?" she asked.

"No, no, it's feeling better. Thank you." She smiled in acknowledgement and continued her examination. The swelling had decreased and she began probing his ankle with her fingers. Henri winced.

"Move your toes for me," she said. He complied.

"Does that hurt?"

He shook his head. It did hurt a little but not enough to admit. Finishing her examination, she straightened up and declared, "It does not appear that you have broken any bones. You were lucky, m'sieur. But you do have a bad sprain. You will need to keep this ankle elevated for a few days. No walking on it." She perched on the table next to his foot. "Why were you so frightened when you thought I was going to Augment you?" He met her gaze somberly.

"I do not want to be a mechanical man, Adelaide. I see those poor blighters in the streets, the veterans with their broken-down parts that no-one cares about anymore. I would rather be missing a limb than have a mechanical one."

"But why? The Augmentations make people stronger and faster. Our Augmented soldiers have made France unconquerable all these years. We have not perfected the Augmentations yet, and yes, they do break down over time, but don't you see? They herald a new age for mankind. We are using artificial means to accelerate natural progress and to compensate for the disadvantages of nature. We are no longer limited by our weak, mortal flesh."

"I happen to like weak, mortal flesh," Henri responded

with a crooked grin. Adelaide blushed and looked away.

Her cheeks turn a lovely shade of pink when she was embarrassed.

"You, *monsieur*, are a libertine," she said, her tone not as severe as her words.

"Ah, but I think you might like libertines," he replied, sliding along the table closer to where she sat. She sputtered at that but no coherent words came out of her mouth. He edged his hand around her corseted waist and stole a quick kiss on that lush mouth. She jumped off the table with an "oh!" and moved away, flushing even deeper. Henri boomed with laughter.

"Tell me, sweet Adelaide, do your automatons kiss you with such warmth?" He noticed her darting a glance at a covered figure lying on a nearby table.

"My automatons? Kiss me? Oh, you scoundrel! The very idea!"

"So you admit that real humans are good for something, something that automatons cannot do?" he teased. She shook her head, confusion on her face. Her unruly hair fell in her eyes. Adelaide tucked it behind her ears and crossed her arms.

"They may not be sensual and warm but machines can be beautiful. They are precise and efficient, symmetrical and clean. The way each part fits its counterpart so cleanly, perfectly, the smoothness of a well-oiled mechanism . . . " She seemed enraptured, passionate and Henri found himself stirred by her words. She picked up the baton she had used on his ankle. "Henri, look at this little device, see how perfectly it fits together; there is no excess, no spare parts. It is completely symmetrical. It must be in order to function. Can you not see the beauty in its form and function?"

Henri slowly nodded his head.

"It is beautiful in its own way, I suppose. But what of life? That mysterious spark of life? What of humanity and our drive for creation? What machine has that? Machines do not think or feel or create. They only do what their creators design them to do." At that, Adelaide glanced away and a small smile appeared on her lips. "That may soon change. How are you getting home, Monsieur Desjardins?"

Henri shrugged. "I thought to take the train back to Paris."

She frowned and shook her head. "Impossible. You can't walk that far on your injured ankle. Have you a friend with a carriage who can fetch you?"

Henri crooked an eyebrow at that. "Madame, I am a poor painter as are my friends. We do not have carriages. Lend me a crutch and I'll hobble down to the station."

Adelaide was silent, chewing her lip. Henri shifted off the table and stood on one leg.

"No! Sit back down. You'll hurt yourself!" She huffed. "I can't have you injure yourself further. I will have to take you home in my new electric carriage."

ഋ Φ ൽ

Adelaide's electric carriage was waiting at a side entrance of the Palace when she helped Henri limp down the broad marble steps. She had given him a sturdy wooden stick since his ankle was still weak. He held it in one hand and braced himself as he descended. She held his other arm. It was warm and firm. She looked up at him and saw his face locked in a grimace of pain. Adelaide felt an unexpected surge of tenderness. She had missed human contact since leaving home to attend the Academy years ago. Her colleagues always seemed cold and unemotional, disdaining idle chatter and physical contact. Some of the men had married but that was frowned upon. And it was strictly forbidden for women Scientists to marry.

Scientists are meant to be focused on our work, removed from human society so that we can remain objective. But sometimes, it's so hard.

Adelaide knew the edicts and understood why they were in place, but it was difficult to stay apart from other people. Especially when they teased her to make her laugh and blush. And especially when their arm felt so nice linked with hers.

She helped Henri up the folding steps onto the seat of the little carriage. It was built to hold two people and resembled a curricle with the driver sitting next to the passenger. The carriage was made of polished wood with a metal frame and sat open to the elements, high above the ground on large carriage wheels. Adelaide was quite pleased with her acquisition. It allowed her to travel around Paris quickly and easily, though people stared as she drove by since there weren't many such vehicles around.

Henri sat down and scrutinized the machine. "Astonishing. It is so little. How does it have enough power to move itself without a large boiler? And where are the funnels? I've seen steam-powered carriages and omnibuses in Paris, but they're large, ungainly. I hate the way they belch smoke and steam as they barrel through the streets."

Adelaide smiled and patted the steering handle in the front affectionately.

"This little beauty runs on electric power. The power supply is right under us. I merely crank the electric motor and it runs for an hour or more, pushing along the carriage.

Are you ready to fly?"

She pulled on long leather gauntlets and tied on a large hat with a veil swathing her face then pushed a button next to the steering handle. The veil hid the grin crossing her face.

ꟃ Φ ꟃ

Henri felt rather than heard the humming from below their seat. Adelaide pushed a lever away from her and the machine moved forward. Henri gripped the hand rail next to him and inhaled sharply. He cast a quick look at Adelaide. She was concentrating on steering the little electric carriage away from the Palace steps. As they turned onto the drive, she pushed the lever further and their speed picked up. The wind rushed past and Henri gasped.

"Adelaide! Are you not going a little fast?" She tossed her head back and laughed.

"Wait until we reach the main Paris road! We can go even faster then!" Henri was silent at that.

Faster? Was she serious?

He felt as if he would blow off the top of the carriage if they went any faster. He darted another look at her. She was smiling, looking as if she had not a care in the world. They turned onto the road to Paris and, as promised, she pushed the lever to speed up the carriage even more. Henri squinted his eyes against the road dirt flying into his face and tugged his hat lower on his head. He found himself enjoying the sensation of speed, the wind ruffling his hair and beard. The light was golden, waning. Henri was surprised at how late it was.

The journey back to Paris seemed to fly by and soon enough Adelaide was picking her way through the streets of Montmartre. The little carriage seemed to have no trouble climbing the steep hills. He directed her to the *hôtel* where his apartment was. He gestured to the building

"I live at the very top of that building. I must have the light, you know," he told her as they clambered down from her electric carriage. Adelaide unwound herself from her veiling but left her driving hat on. He winced as his injured ankle took his weight again and he braced himself with the walking stick.

She must have noticed his flinch because she offered him her arm. He took it gratefully. They proceeded to slowly climb the dozen flights of stairs up to his studio, Henri wincing and gasping. The stairwell was dark and rank with the smell of cabbage and tobacco. Henri held on to the rickety hand rail as he climbed. His ankle was throbbing again when they finally reached the top. Henri fumbled with his key in the dim light. He got the door open after a few moments and staggered inside, relieved to be home. With a groan, he flung himself down on the chaise where he normally posed his models.

"Oh this wretched ankle of mine. My dear Adelaide, I am afraid that your cunning scientific treatment of my injured ankle was all for naught as I fear it is once again grievously swollen." Adelaide bustled about, lighting the wall sconces. She placed her hat and veil on a stool, then came over to his side, kneeling down.

"Let me see," she said. He allowed her to pull up his trouser leg and remove his sock and shoe. The ankle was indeed swollen again and purple-black with bruising. He contemplated it woefully.

"You will need to keep this ankle up for a few days, Henri. No climbing up and down those stairs, understand?

Now what do we have here that can take down this swelling?" Her gaze swept around the studio, noticing the mess for the first time. "Henri, this room is unsanitary. Is that a cheese rind on the floor? I am sure you must have rats in here." He blushed, a little shame-faced and replied,

"I am afraid I am not much of a housekeeper. You must realize, I am an artist, and so I rise above the mundane. Also, I do not have the money to pay someone to clean for me." She rolled her eyes and got up, walking to the sink. Adelaide pumped some water on to her handkerchief then brought it back. She knelt next to him, head at his knee and laid the wet handkerchief across his ankle.

"I wish I had brought my tools with me. I could have treated your ankle again." He smiled and put his hand on hers. She looked up at him, smiling in return.

"I deeply appreciate all of your assistance, Adelaide. I am not certain how I would have made it home without you." He rubbed the top of her hand slowly and gently with his thumb.

ꕥ Φ ꕥ

Adelaide sat very still, enjoying the sensation. He sat up and tugged her hand so she came closer to him. He took hold of her shoulders and slowly drew her closer still, holding her gaze. She didn't object. He put his mouth on hers and tenderly kissed her. She shivered and his kiss deepened, his arms going around her. She kissed him back eagerly and returned his embrace. They broke their kiss, both panting a little. She felt her face flush and watched him from under heavy eyelids, waiting for his next move.

There was a knock at the door. Startled, she pulled out of his arms and stood up.

"Should I get that?" she asked. Henri started to shake his head then they heard a woman's voice on the other side of the door.

"Henri? Are you there? Your lights are on. Let me in," she called. Adelaide was shaken.

Who was that? His wife? Mistress?

"You stay there and rest your ankle. I will get the door for you," she said. She walked over to the door, skirts swaying, head held high. Adelaide opened the door and stepped to the side.

ꙮ Φ ꙮ

Henri saw Isabelle standing in the doorway, pulling a puzzled face when she spotted the stranger in Henri's studio. Adelaide in her plain, black gown obviously wasn't one of Henri's typical subjects. Isabelle swept into the room and spotted Henri lounging on the chaise.

"Henri?" she said, clearly hoping for some sort of explanation. Henri groaned melodramatically and gestured at his ankle.

"Isabelle, look! I have injured myself! The good doctor here tells me that my ankle is badly sprained and I cannot walk on it." Isabelle scowled at Henri then Adelaide, who nodded in confirmation.

"Oh? And how did you hurt yourself? And where did this . . . doctor . . . come from? Madame?"

"Monsieur Desjardins was strolling in the gardens of Versailles when he apparently tripped on a tree root and twisted his ankle. I was summoned since I was the closest doctor. I have done what I can but he must elevate the injury and refrain from walking for at least three days," Adelaide replied. Henri was avoiding meeting Adelaide's eye.

Isabelle glared at Adelaide, head held high. "You have our thanks, Madame. What is your fee?"

Adelaide shook her head. "No, no fee is needed. I was merely doing my civic duty to aid an injured citizen. Now, I must bid you both a good night. Please stay off that ankle, m'sieur." She fetched her hat and driving veil and was gone before Henri could think of something to say.

"So our good doctor even brought you home, Henri?" Isabelle asked, eyebrow arched. Henri nodded, his eyes on Adelaide's handkerchief still draped across his ankle. "How very civil of her. Well, since you are injured, I will not stay. You need your rest, according to the good doctor. *Bon nuit*, Henri." She flounced out the door, banging it behind her. Henri let his head drop back on to the pillow.

Oh dear. That was rather awkward. What dreadful timing.

His stomach rumbled.

And I was hoping Isabelle would bring me dinner.

Henri limped around the studio, dousing the lights and went to bed, hungry and alone.

Eight

The morning air was still chilly, despite the sun shining brightly over the rooftops of Montmartre. Adelaide stood in front of the dilapidated hôtel where Henri lived, holding a fresh baguette. Her impulse to venture to his studio to check on his ankle seemed misguided, even foolish now that she had arrived. She was out of place here in this artists' haven.

He might be sleeping. That woman might be there still, sharing his bed. She had seemed very proprietary last night.

Henri had told Adelaide that he was unmarried but he neglected to say whether he had a mistress.

And didn't all these artistic types have mistresses?

Housewives, laden with market baskets were the only people out this early. They ogled at her curiously as she stood there in her black silk gown, obviously new and expensive. The women in this arrondissement were a little shabby, their dresses worn and faded.

I should leave, go back to the Palace where I belong, she

told herself. She spun back around to her little electric curricle.

Back to the Palace. Where no-one ever touches me or even looks at me as if I were a person.

Adelaide paused, torn between her fear of being in the wrong place and, she had to admit, an undeniable desire to see Henri.

I'll regret this if I just leave.

Determined, she swung back around to face building and marched up to the door. It was ajar. She pushed it open further and peeked inside. The foyer was deserted and surprisingly clean but she spotted no sign of a concierge. Emboldened, she stepped inside and headed for the stairs.

"Madame!" a sharp voice called out from an alcove she hadn't noticed. Adelaide froze. "May I be of assistance, Madame?" A small, hunched woman in grey hobbled out of the alcove and cast a suspicious glare at Adelaide. "I am the concierge here. How may I help you?"

Adelaide's stomach churned with nervousness and her sense of being out of place. She tilted her head at the little woman and pretending to imperious Scientist arrogance that she didn't feel, replied, "I thank you, Madame, but I do not require your assistance. I am here to visit the painter Henri Desjardins and know where to find him."

With that, Adelaide swept up the stairs leaving the concierge to glower after her retreating back. She climbed and climbed, trying to ignore the stench of mold and old cooking. She had to watch her footing on the uneven stairs and torn carpet. Reaching the top, Adelaide halted to catch her breath. She smoothed back her hair. Adjusted her clothing. Taking a deep breath, she approached the door and softly, tentatively knocked. No answer. She waited before knocking again, a little louder this time. She took another breath but her courage deserted her.

Adelaide spun around and had reached the top of the stairs when she heard Henri's door open. She glanced back over her shoulder. Henri stood in the doorway leaning on the borrowed walking stick and yawning, looking more rumpled than usual.

"Adelaide? Am I dreaming? Have you come to give me succor in my hour of need, my darling doctor?"

"I—I brought you fresh bread. I wanted to . . . to check on you—on your ankle," she stammered, feeling the blush suffusing her face.

Grinning, he gestured for her to enter his studio, then followed her in, closing the door firmly and locking it. He hobbled to his divan using the walking stick, sitting down with a thump. He grimaced.

"Please, m'sieur, you must keep your foot elevated," Adelaide reminded him. He swung his leg up onto the divan, shooting a glare at Adelaide from under his bushy eyebrows. She moved closer to take a look at his injury. His feet were bare and he wore loose linen pants with a half-open shirt.

They must be his bed clothes . . . or something he just threw on after getting out of bed.

The thought made her feel awkward, like an intruder into an intimate place. She could see sparse, curly dark hair on his chest through the open placket of his shirt and became even more flustered. She dropped her eyes and kneeled to examine his ankle, rather than his partially naked chest. Henri watched her, seeming to be amused at her modesty and embarrassment.

"Does my *déshabillé* offend you, my sweet Adelaide?" he purred. She refused to look up, instead shaking her head silently. She suddenly realized that she was still holding the baguette, clutching it so tightly that the crust crackled under her fingers. In a rush, she pushed it at him.

"Your bread. Here," she said. Henri grinned, taking it from her.

"Merci. You are too kind, dearest Adelaide. However did you guess that I had not a bite to eat last night and that there is absolutely no bread in my humble living quarters?" He broke off a piece and started chewing, making little sounds of pleasure as he chewed. "Ah, if only I had a jug of wine as well, for I already have thou." She didn't reply, choosing instead to prod his bruised ankle. He wiggled his toes and said, "You see, the swelling has much decreased. Your excellent treatment has almost cured me. I attribute it to your lovely little handkerchief which you so gently laid across it before disappearing into the dark night."

With an effort, Adelaide regained her composure and said briskly, "Good, good. So the pain too has decreased? You are able to walk?"

He grasped her hand and she glanced at it, then at him.

"Yes. How can I thank you for your kind ministrations, my sweet Adelaide?" His smile was teasing and warm. He began to caress her bare wrist between her glove and her sleeve. She shivered and tried to pull her hand away. He refused to let her go and pulled off her glove then brought her hand up to his lips. Gazing into her eyes, he kissed her hand slowly and softly, letting his breath warm her skin between his kisses.

"What—what are you doing?" she muttered.

"I am trying to see if your skin is as sweet as you are," he responded. Adelaide recalled that it was entirely scandalous for her to be here alone in this man's apartment. And now he was removing her other glove to cover her other hand with those tiny, soft kisses. He moved on to kissing her palms. She knew she should object but her body felt languorous and weak, her gaze trapped by his.

"Adelaide," he groaned and released her hands to draw her into his arms. She let him pull her down against him. His chest felt hot, even through the layers of silk and cotton she was wearing. His hand came up and grabbed the back of her neck and then his mouth was on hers, hot and wet and demanding. Adelaide lost herself in the sensation of his kisses. Her body felt as if it were on fire and she welcomed his hands opening the buttons on the front of her bodice, then pushing it apart to let the air flow over her skin. She shrugged out of the tight-fitting bodice and his hands ran up and down her bare arms.

He unfastened her skirt and pushed it down to her hips. He pulled his mouth off of hers and quickly, seemingly with some experience, he unclasped the busk on her corset. She exhaled with relief as the constraint was removed from her waist and chest. Slowly, and tentatively, he ran his hands around her rib cage to her back, running his hands up and down her spine before drawing her into his arms to kiss her once more. She moaned quietly against his mouth as he kissed her. He gently cupped her breast, almost naked now but for her thin lawn chemise. Adelaide felt the heat from his hand through the fabric and trembled. Finally, he stood her up and drew the rest of her garments from her, leaving her standing completely nude in front of him. He surveyed her form, hands around her waist before swinging her on to the divan. He quickly stripped off his own clothes and knelt between her parted legs. She couldn't think anymore, waiting for the next irresistible sensation.

ꟹ Φ ☙

Sometime later, Henri stretched his arms above his head.

"You are an incredibly passionate woman, Adelaide. You are so...human." Adelaide cocked her head and smiled.

"Did you expect an automaton?" she asked, her voice light and teasing. He avoided her eyes, frowning slightly. "You did! You thought I was Augmented!"

"Perhaps. I expected a Scientist-Doctor to take advantage of the modifications available." She shook her head.

"I may work on automatons but I have no need of Augmentation. My body is strong and healthy." She smiled seductively at him. "You felt how strong and healthy my body is, did you not?" He growled a little and bent down to kiss her bared nipple.

"Oh, yes. Very strong and healthy. Healthy enough for more of this?" He continued to lick her nipple and she moved under him. "Let us move to a more comfortable spot." He swept her up off the divan and carried her into his darkened bedroom, not limping at all.

ꟹ Φ ☙

Adelaide wasn't sure how long she had been lying in Henri's bed, being pleasured. They had eaten after calling down to the concierge for some food from the local bistro and fell asleep for a while. The light waned when she finally woke.

"Henri. I must go," she said. He grumbled a little then stirred, wrapping a hairy arm around her waist.

"No. You just arrived," he muttered. She giggled.

"It has been hours. I must return to the Palace. I have so

much to do," she told him. Fully awake now, he regarded her.

"What is so important that you must leave our bed of bliss, my lovely Adelaide?" His sweet words made her smile.

"My work must be completed before the King . . ." she stopped herself, wary of saying too much.

"The King is waiting for your work? Is it an Augmentation for him?"

"No, not exactly. It will replace him." She winced. She didn't mean to let that slip out but she felt so relaxed she couldn't help herself.

"Replace the King? Do you mean replace him with a mechanical person, some kind of automaton?"

Her feeling of languor left her and her stomach tensed. She shouldn't have let that slip. Adelaide glanced at Henri. He raised himself up on his elbow and stared down at her. "Adelaide, you can't do that, you can't replace the King with an automaton. It would not be natural. It would not be right. It would be an abomination."

She sat up, clutching his grubby sheet to her chest. "Don't be melodramatic, Henri. Automation is not an abomination. It is an improvement."

Henri shook his head vigorously. "We do not need more automatons in France, Adelaide, we need fewer. These cyborg monarchs of yours need to be replaced. We need new blood in our monarchy, human blood, not more mechanical men."

Adelaide was still, coldness creeping into her. Henri was talking treason. Replacing the monarchs? She drew a breath and climbed out of the bed.

"Henri, I must go. I am sorry," she said. His face reddened and his mouth drooped. He gazed out the window, not meeting her eyes. She left the room and dressed quickly in the studio, then slipped out and was gone.

ꟈ Φ ꟈ

Adelaide walked into her empty, darkened laboratory. It was evening. She'd spent the entire day in Henri Desjardins' bed, neglecting her duties here. Now that the thrill of his seduction was over, she found herself regretting her actions. How could she have allowed him to seduce her? She had violated the code of ethics that she had sworn to when accepting the mantle of Scientist. Adelaide sat down in a chair behind her desk in a niche. She had let her senses take over. She had lost control and engaged in immoral behavior.

And what if I am with child?

She bit her lip, still swollen from Henri's many kisses. How could she have lost control like that? She had remained virginal for thirty years, untouched and untempted. What was it about Henri that had wrecked that self-control?

Henri, the libertine!

She ran her hand lightly along the collar of her bodice, enjoying the sensation, remembering his fingers doing the same. But was Henri a traitor? His words were treasonous but were they just words? Was he a traitor in actions as well? Perhaps he had seduced her to infiltrate her laboratory. She frowned. Adelaide thought about him sitting on the examining table in her laboratory. She didn't remember if anything confidential had been visible while he sat there. And had he looked around, like a spy would? She couldn't recall.

The Automated Dauphin had been covered, she knew. She got up to look over at the table on which her creation lay then sat back down in her niche. She always kept him covered when not working on him. Thank goodness for that. She still didn't want anyone seeing him. It was too soon. With a start, she recalled her slip about the King when she was in Henri's bed. She groaned and let her head fall into her hands.

If Henri were truly a traitor, that slip could be disastrous. How could I have been so foolish? Was I so charmed by him that I lost all control?

Her breath caught in her chest at the thought. Her heart pounded. Then she shook her head and took a deep breath to calm herself. Don't be ridiculous, Adelaide, she told herself. He's just a painter, a painter obsessed with the natural world. He can do no harm to the monarchy.

The room was almost fully dark now, the heavy curtains drawn against the deepening twilight. She hadn't eaten since breakfasting with Henri.

I should probably ring for a tray. I wonder if someone brought Henri something more to eat in his garret.

The door clicked open quietly as she sat there. She didn't react, still wrapped up in her own thoughts. Someone flicked on a small electric light in the main part of the laboratory, grabbing her attention. Adelaide couldn't see from where she was sitting at her desk in the niche. She rose and thought to call to whoever was there but paused. Why hadn't the person switched on the main lights? That meant that something stealthy was going on in her laboratory. Could it be Henri, following her back to the Palace? Or a saboteur from the Naturalist Underground?

Quietly, Adelaide rose from her chair and peeked around the corner. It was Zoé. Relieved, she opened her mouth to speak but noticed that Zoé stood beside the Automated Dauphin. The girl held a tool. Adelaide watched and saw her snipping something in the torso of the automaton and removed a part.

What is she doing? Repair work? We hadn't discussed anything of the sort.

Zoé picked up a small hammer and banged on the excised part until Adelaide heard it smash. That was no late evening repair, she was sabotaging the Automated Dauphin. Her trusted assistant was sabotaging her work.

Adelaide felt sick then a rush of anger entered her body, leaving her trembling. She stepped out of the niche and quietly said, "Zoé. You treacherous baggage. Drop that tool immediately." Zoé started violently and turned, eyes wide in the bright light of her portable light.

"Madame Le Professeur! You startled me. I was—I was repairing—"

"I saw exactly what you were doing, you disgusting little luddite. You were sabotaging my creation. Destroying my life work. And I wager it was not the first time. The arterial connector problem? I am going to hazard a guess that it was due to your sabotage, not a problem with the design."

Zoé shook her head frantically. "No, no, it is not true. I would never—" Adelaide quickly moved closer to her and when she reached her side, grabbed her wrist, squeezing it hard. Zoé dropped the tool and stood there shaking.

"You are lying!" Adelaide shouted. The girl continued to deny her wrongdoing, shaking her head repeatedly. Adelaide slapped her hard across the face. "You have betrayed me! You are a lying weasel and I will see you in prison for this." She dropped Zoé's hand and marched to the door, flinging it open.

"Guards!" she screamed. "Guards! There is a traitor in my laboratory!" Guards ran down the hallway, their footsteps thundering on the wood floor. Two burly men in uniform squeezed past Adelaide standing in the doorway and seized the shaking, weeping Zoé. As they dragged the girl away, Adelaide pulled the captain of the guards aside.

"There is another traitor. You must go to Montmartre and arrest the painter Henri Desjardins. He has admitted to me that he is a seditionist, devoted to overthrowing the monarchy. He must not be allowed to infect the populace with his treacherous words." The captain nodded his assent and the troops left, dragging Zoé out of the room. Adelaide began to shake harder as she returned to her laboratory and closed the door. She slid down the door and sat against it, wrapping her arms around herself. Hot, bitter tears escaped her closed lids.

"I am sorry, Henri," she said to the empty room. "I had to do it. I cannot allow anyone to threaten my work."

Nine

The lights were unlit in Henri's studio. Henri was sitting on the sill of an open window, watching people in the lighted street below. He was feeling relaxed but somehow melancholy. Isabelle sauntered into Henri's studio, carrying a basket.

"Henri, are you looking for something to paint out there?" Isabelle said gaily. "I brought dinner." He glanced over at her.

"*Bon soir*, Isabelle. It is so kind of you to feed me," he said quietly. Isabelle tilted her head at his tone.

"Are you feeling well, Henri? You do not sound yourself at all. Is your ankle still paining you?"

"No, no, my ankle is feeling fine. I am just hungry." He pushed himself off the sill and came across the room to embrace her. He stepped away from the embrace quickly and tried to take her basket but she pulled it away.

"I do not even get a kiss for bringing you a pot of Madame Leguire's famous cassoulet?" Henri obediently kissed her. She wrinkled her nose at his perfunctory kiss and went to light the wall sconce lamps.

"Never mind, I will not get anything until you are fed, I see." She shivered and glanced around at the studio. "Why are the windows open? It is freezing in here."

"It was stuffy. And it smelled bad." Isabelle's eyebrows shot up as she crossed the room to close the windows against the chill of the night air. It had started to rain and the windowsills were wet.

"And when does it not smell bad in here?" she asked. She examined the cluttered studio. "You have tidied up. Well, at least you got rid of the wine bottles and old food."

"It was unsanitary," he replied. Isabelle laughed outright, choking out,

"Unsanitary? Since when do you care about that?"

Henri didn't laugh in return. Adelaide had been quite disgusted by the squalor of his home and he had felt compelled to clean it. Isabelle shook her head and unpacked the basket of food, bringing out a covered pot and some bowls. "Come on, let me feed you and then perhaps you will start to make sense."

They devoured the hot savory cassoulet without speaking. He gazed at Isabelle, her curly dark hair falling down her back. She hated wearing it up, said all those pins hurt her head. He loved running his hands through that hair but found himself remembering Adelaide constantly pushing tendrils of her light brown hair off her face He mentally shook himself, trying to remain present here with Isabelle. She ate with gusto, gravy smeared across her thick, plump lips. He adored kissing those lips and her smooth tawny skin. He found himself getting aroused, despite the long vigorous day he had spent loving Adelaide.

Isabelle flashed her eyes up and spotted his lustful look. She smiled and reached out to stroke the side of his face.

He turned his head towards her hand and kissed it, feeling the roughness of her work-roughened palm. The smell of laundry soap clung to her skin. Henri finished his meal and reached out for her. She daintily wiped her mouth on a cloth and put her food aside. Moving into his waiting arms, she murmured, "Now that is more like my Henri."

He kissed her hard in response but his hands rested on her back and he didn't hold her close. Henri tried to push aside a welling up of guilt. He and Isabelle weren't exclusive. Or rather, he had other dalliances. He wasn't so sure about Isabelle. She seemed to always be available to him and often visited his studio unannounced. He was lucky that she hadn't encountered another of his lady loves. Adelaide's body had been pale and thin when she'd lain naked in his bed, allowing him to introduce her to the mysteries of love. He felt queerly tender towards her at the thought. Isabelle pulled away, sensing his lack of attention to their kiss.

"Henri, you are so distant? What are you thinking of? Is it that scientist lady who was here last night?" she intuited. How could she even guess that, thought Henri. He tried to school his face and appear nonchalant.

"Ah . . . Madame Le Professeur was very helpful to me yesterday when I injured myself," he said. She scrutinized his face and her eyes widened with disbelief.

"Helpful? Ha! Is that what you are calling it? I thought those scientists were pledged to be chaste? Did she break her vows for you, Henri?" She shoved away from him, mouth twisted in scorn.

Henri recoiled, he hadn't thought of Adelaide's Scientist vows when he had so blithely seduced her.

"No, no, I didn't...we ..." he stuttered. Isabelle laughed, a little bitterly, clearly not believing his claim of innocence.

"Well, well, the famed seducer Henri Desjardins managed to get one of those uptight Scientists into his bed. So how much of her was human and how much mechanical?"

"She is not Augmented!" He burst out, then realized that he had admitted to bedding Adelaide. Isabelle bit her full lower lip, making it redder than before.

"So you did bed her. Oh, Henri. How could you?" Her brown eyes welled with tears. Henri dropped his head, shame filling him.

"I'm sorry, Isabelle. I had to." His voice was quiet, without its usual gaiety.

"You had to bed the Scientist lady? What? What do you mean? Was she irresistible?"

"No, no. It was an assignment, Isabelle, but it is best if you know no more. I don't want you to get in trouble." Henri took her into his arms again. She refused to meet his eyes. "Please believe me when I tell you that I had to seduce her and that this is a dangerous game I am playing. One I do not want you involved in. If anything should happen, you will be safer if you know nothing more than that." She brought her eyes to meet his, upset still writ on her face.

"You are being mysterious again, Henri. Does this have to do with the movement you are involved in? Bringing a natural monarch back to France?" He nodded. "Henri, you are right, this is dangerous ground you are treading. How do you know this Scientist will not betray you?"

"Betray me? What do you mean?"

Isabelle's face was grave with concern. "You seduced a Scientist, vowed to chastity. That is high treason, Henri. Or did your mysterious Underground connection fail to inform you of that?" Henri felt a cold sinking feeling in his gut.

"She would not . . . would not betray me," he said, uncertainty coloring his tone.

"Are you sure about that, mon cher?" Isabelle asked, gazing into his eyes. Henri nodded, pushing aside his worry. He smiled, mouth crooked and reached out to her, cupping her face.

"Will you forgive me, ma petite? It was not my idea. I deeply regret having to betray you."

She pouted a little, drawing out the reconciliation.

"It was unkind of you to worry me, Henri."

"I know and I am sorry. Come, it is getting late. Let us go to bed." They got up from their impromptu picnic on the floor. Isabelle put the dishes back in her basket.

A loud hammering shook the door. The couple jumped, Isabelle uttering a little cry. A loud voice from the other side of the door bellowed,

"Henri Desjardins! Open in the name of the law!" Henri froze, unable to breathe for a moment. He and Isabelle exchanged glances.

"Go. Go into the bedroom, ma chère," he told her. She scurried to the bedroom but stood in the doorway, watching Henri with wide eyes. He shook his head and gestured her to move into the other room. She stepped out of view.

Taking a trembling breath, Henri moved towards the door. Whoever stood outside was impatient and hammered on the door again. Henri turned the knob and fell back as four men on the other side pushed it open. They were Police Secrète, judging by their dark grey uniforms. Henri felt his legs tremble and nearly toppled to the side. His injured ankle seemed to weaken again as the officers advanced upon him. He could hear the whirring of the policemen's Augmented limbs.

"How may I be of assistance, officers?" he asked, trying

to be calm. The captain of the patrol stared hard at him, frowning.

"Are you Henri Desjardins of Montmartre, a painter?"

"Yes, that is I." The police officers closed around him, taking hold of his arms with inhuman strength as the captain declaimed,

"Henri Desjardins, you are hereby arrested for the high crime of treason." Henri's body involuntarily jerked at those words and he cried out. One of the police officers spun him around and summarily shackled him with heavy iron bands.

This can't be happening. Adelaide wouldn't do this. Would she?

"Who accuses me of this heinous offense?" he demanded, holding his head high, his heart hammering in his ears.

The captain sneered at him. "A high ranking Court official brought the charges upon you."

Henri was stunned. He had never been involved in the Court and the only Court official he knew was Adelaide. Adelaide had accused him? That meant that Isabelle had been right. The policeman tightened the bands and yanked at his prisoner's arms. Henri glimpsed Isabelle standing at the bedroom door, murder in her eyes. She mouthed at him, *I knew it*. Henri nodded, feeling terror grip his throat as his legs turned to jelly. He whimpered under his breath and tried to pull away from the officer but the Augmented man was too strong. Henri was held fast. One of the officer's colleagues turned and backhanded Henri across the face then stepped in closer and gut punched him. Henri felt the breath forced from his body and he doubled over, groaning. The officer let him drop to the floor. Henri fell on his face, unable to catch himself.

How could Adelaide have done this to him? After their sweet, sweet day of love. He thought she had understood how important the natural world was.

The captain stepped up to Henri and kicked him in the stomach.

“On your feet, you seditious scum.”

Henri struggled to get up but couldn’t brace himself. Sedition. His chest tightened when he realized the severity of the charge. Treason was punishable by execution. He could lose his life over some Scientist's virginity. As he lay on the ground, he silently berated himself for his naiveté. The police officers hauled him to his feet and with one on each side, moved him towards the door. Henri didn’t resist, his head spinning.

“No!” Isabelle cried, and run towards him, flinging her arms around him. One of the officers grabbed her long hair and flung her to the ground. Henri lurched towards her, but his captors held him fast.

“ISABELLE!” he bellowed.

A hand clamped over his mouth and they dragged him quickly out of the door, leaving Isabelle sobbing on the dusty floor of his studio.

ꕥ Φ ꕥ

Early morning light streamed in through the high windows of John's studio. He sat sketching Marie-Ange's face from memory, his charcoal lovingly dwelling on her features, her rosebud mouth, her high forehead, her wide, round eyes. He scowled. The resemblance wasn’t quite right.

The cold room sought his skin, but he kept warm and

comfortable in his thick brocade and velvet robe, a recent acquisition. The duchesse de Fronsac had paid well so he allowed himself this little indulgence. He stroked the robe, liking the way the fabric felt under his fingertips.

He heard footsteps approaching then someone hammered on the door. He was not expecting anyone at such an early hour. Puzzled, he put aside his sketch pad and went to open the door. It was Isabelle. Her face was swollen and blotchy and her eyes were rimmed with red.

"John! You must help me!" she gasped out. Alarmed, he urged her inside and shut the door behind her. She immediately burst into tears. He pulled out his handkerchief and handed it to her. She held it but made no move to use it.

"Isabelle, are you hurt? What's wrong?" he asked. She shook her head and mumbled something incoherent through her tears. He led her to his parlor. He directed the sobbing woman to a chair by a window, removed her cloak and helped her sit. In the better light, he could see her more clearly. Her hair was disheveled and the bodice of her dress was askew and puckered. It appeared to be fastened incorrectly. He didn't see any bruises or blood but perhaps she was injured under her clothing. He knelt in front of her and took her cold hand, chafing it with his.

Her sobs quieted after a little while. She gazed down at John, eyes filled with tears, and said, "Henri . . . Henri was . . . arrested." She sobbed once and started to shake, her hand pressed to her mouth. John felt his body go cold under the thick robe and got to his feet.

"Henri was arrested? What happened, Isabelle? You must tell me more."

"The Police Secrète came to his studio last night and arrested him. They said he was a traitor. Oh, John, they execute traitors, don't they?"

John shook his head in disbelief. Had Henri's idle words finally got him into trouble? Who would have reported him? Paris was crawling with spies but how many seditious conversations did it take for the Police Secrète to actually arrest someone?

"Isabelle, did they say what he had done?"

"Please, John, you must help him. You have connections at Court. Maybe you could ask one of them for help? They can't execute him!"

"Now, now, don't jump to conclusions; we do not know what is happening. Perhaps they will simply question him and when they learn that he is innocent, he will be released." Isabelle's eyes were big and tragic as she shook her head.

"Henri talks a lot but he is innocent of treason," John said. "Am I correct?"

"I don't think he was arrested for speaking out against the monarchy. He told me about this lady Scientist . . ." she stopped, her lower lip trembling. "He seduced her."

John felt his heart sink. How could Henri be so stupid as to seduce a lady Scientist?

"That is why he was arrested? This Scientist spoke out against him?"

Isabelle nodded, her mouth downturned in misery. John groaned and got up. He paced back and forth, feeling Isabelle's eyes watching him.

"Please, John, you must help him," she begged.

John stopped pacing and stood at a window, looking out so as not to meet her eyes.

"I am afraid there is nothing I can do. This is beyond my control."

Isabelle cried out in protest. She stood up and walked to his side. "John, please, you must try to save Henri. There must be someone you can talk to. We cannot let him be executed." She placed her hand on his upper arm. He contemplated her hand but still didn't meet her eyes. Henri was his brother and the first friend he had made in Paris. The notion of him being imprisoned and executed for indulging in his sensual nature saddened John. A thought occurred to him.

Why, with all the women in Paris, would he choose to seduce a lady Scientist?

"Isabelle, where did he meet this woman? Scientists are not in Henri's usual circles." Isabelle didn't answer. John could see a flush creeping across her cheeks under her tawny color.

"I do not know where they met," she responded without meeting his eyes.

Why is she lying to me? What is going on here?

Isabelle did not appear to be jealous of Henri's affaire with this lady Scientist; it seemed like there was something more. Gently, John raised her chin to force her to look into his eyes.

"Isabelle. You must tell me the whole story."

"Will you promise to help get Henri out of prison?"

"I cannot promise that. I have little power. If I ask my noble clients for this kind of favor, they would most likely laugh at me and never commission me again."

Isabelle leaned closer to John, wrapped her arm around his neck and kissed him on the mouth softly. Her warm mouth felt exquisite against his, and he deepened the kiss with a groan. She tasted like rich wine and tendrils of desire wound through his body. He pulled back and gazed at her. Her deep brown eyes invited him to continue. The skin of her face and neck resembled warm satin and he was struck by a need to see more of it.

Shaking, he caressed her cheek with just the tips of his fingers. She waited, watching him. Her mouth parted, inviting his kiss. His exploring fingers went into her hair, smoothing it back. It was thick and coarse but felt alive under his fingers. He lowered his mouth back down to hers, wanting to taste more of her. He wrapped his arms around her, realizing as he did that she wasn't wearing a corset under her dress, just some light stays. Her body felt soft and yielding against his as her lush curves pressed against him.

John gasped with desire, shaking. He needed to have her. With trembling fingers, he unfastened a few buttons on the front of her bodice, drawing in a breath sharply when he reached the satin-smooth skin over her collarbone. Her skin glowed in the sunlight and he paused to admire it. He dropped delicate kisses down her throat and along her collarbone. She moaned softly at the sensation. At the sound, husky and deep, he stopped. This was Isabelle. He couldn't make love to Isabelle, as desperate as he was to feel her under him. Even if she and Henri weren't exclusive, what about Marie-Ange? Using every ounce of his self-control, he pulled away, out of her arms.

"I—I apologize, Isabelle. I do not know what possessed me. Please—please forgive me," he stammered. He stepped away from her and began pacing, trying to calm himself.

"I see. So you will not help me?" she asked, buttoning up her bodice. He gaped at her. She had been willing to give herself to him to secure assistance with Henri's imprisonment. He wondered if Henri knew how much Isabelle loved him.

"I . . . I will do what I can. I cannot promise anything, but I will do what I can." Isabelle nodded, looking defeated and sad. Tears sprang to her eyes again.

"*Merci*," she said and departed quickly, saying nothing

more. John watched her go, still feeling a burning desire for her lush curves and uninhibited sensuality. He cursed his mental disloyalty to Marie-Ange and picked up his sketch of her. Her lovely features, that delicate nose, porcelain skin, all lovingly drafted just a few short moments ago failed to stir his heart. Would she ever kiss him with abandon? He tried but couldn't imagine her perfect, tranquil face transfixed with pleasure.

ഗ Φ ശ

Marie-Ange entered the enamellers' suite at the Palace, accompanied by Françoise, the duchesse de Fronsac. So many of the Court ladies received enameling treatments that the *Maître* had set aside a series of rooms at the Palace so that the ladies did not have to travel.

"Are you excited to receive your first treatment, ma chère?" Françoise asked. Marie-Ange didn't answer immediately, she was trying to stifle what felt like a flock of butterflies in her belly. She smiled at Françoise.

"I suppose. Are you sure this is appropriate, Madame?"

Françoise patted her arm. "Ma chère, you must call me Françoise or I will feel as old as your dear *maman*. But is this appropriate? To look as beautiful as Her Majesty? Of course, it is appropriate. You wish the Queen to continue to favor you, do you not?"

Marie-Ange nodded. She desperately wanted to please the Queen.

"Well, then, Marie-Ange, emulating her fine complexion is your silent way of honoring Her Majesty."

Françoise turned to the waiting enameller, a man whose dark skin contrasted with his tidy white suit. "Is all in readiness for Mademoiselle de Laincel? You do recall that this is the first time her skin has been enameled? You must use only the most gentle of unguents and potions."

The enameller bowed deeply to the duchesse. "Oui, Madame la Duchesse. I will treat her tender skin with the most exquisite of care as befits such a delicate, young flower."

Marie-Ange was taken aback. She didn't feel particularly like a delicate, young flower. She eyed the loquacious enameller with a hint of suspicion. What exactly was he planning to do to her? She found it odd that a man with such dark skin would be creating pure white faces for the ladies of the Court. She peeked back at Françoise, taking in her smooth, pale complexion that was due to the work of this enameller. The duchess was exquisite.

"Come, come, let us begin," he said. The butterflies were back, and they seemed to have multiplied. Marie-Ange tried to breathe deeply to dispel the feeling but her corset would only let her take in the tiniest gasp of air, certainly not enough to help her relax. The enameller took her by the arm and steered her towards a long chaise raised a few feet above the ground. He helped her climb the steps up to it. She sat down on the edge, feet still on the little steps. She didn't want to lay down. She wasn't sure about doing this after all.

"Ma chère, you must lay down," Françoise said. "Here, let me help you with your skirts. Are you not glad that I told you to leave off the bustle and keep your simple old dress on? You would find it impossible to lay down. There will be time for you to don your lovely new gown after you have been enameled. The Queen is going to be so pleased."

Françoise's rattling speech did little to quell Marie-Ange's nerves. What would her mother say if she knew she was getting her face enameled? She was at home in Aix-en-

Provence but what if she and her father decided to travel to Paris for a visit?

"Françoise, I do not think I should do this. I do not think my mother would approve." Marie-Ange sat up abruptly. Françoise pushed her back down.

"Ma chère, your mother sent you to Paris to serve the Queen. You must fit in with the rest of her ladies-in-waiting. This will please Her Majesty. That is all you need to tell your dear *maman*. Now come, let us proceed."

She stepped back to let the enameller move closer. Marie-Ange could feel the palms of her hands grow moist and she could not quite catch her breath. The enameller moved closer still, holding a rough cloth and a pot of some sort of paste. He smeared it across her face and scrubbed. Marie-Ange held back her gasps of pain as he plucked and pinched at her skin, preparing it for the enamel. He smoothed lotions on and wiped them off with soft cloths. Finally he pulled out a delicate brush and the pot of enamel. He was silent as he painted the enamel on her skin.

"Mademoiselle, you look beautiful, *enchantée*! Your beauty is enhanced beyond that of mere mortals." The enameller brushed one more delicate stroke across Marie-Ange's cheek and stepped back, smiling. He held up a mirror for her inspection.

She started a little, not quite expecting the brilliant white of the enamel, despite being familiar with the enameled faces of the Queen and ladies of the court. It was eerie to see her own blue eyes staring out of the white, still human in a doll's face. She wasn't sure if she liked the effect. The enameller gave her no room for doubt as he fluttered around, making little bird chirps of approval. She tried to smile up at him in return but found that her cheeks were quite frozen, and she could barely move her mouth.

"M'sieur, how am I supposed to eat?" She murmured. Her breathing came a little fast as she realized the extent of her facial paralysis.

"Eat? Ha, how will you fit into your tight gowns if you eat!" Françoise answered for the enameller. "You look beautiful, as I knew you would. Now shall we adjourn to your chambers. There is a new gown waiting there for you." Marie-Ange sat up slowly. The stiffness of her face was disconcerting. Her breathing returned to normal but she started to feel a dull ache in her chest.

Oh, no. Not again.

"I thank you, m'sieur," she said, remembering her manners. She walked slowly out of the room, the pain in her chest growing.

"Françoise. Would you be so kind as to summon Madame Le Professeur. I am feeling a little unwell."

Françoise stared at her with alarm. She took Marie-Ange's arm and helped her to her rooms, ordering a servant to fetch Adelaide. Marie-Age sat down on one of the uncomfortable gilt chairs in her sitting room. She felt dizzy now and didn't want to walk any further. Françoise hovered nearby, not speaking. Adelaide finally arrived carrying her doctor's bag and shooed out the duchesse. The noblewoman scurried out.

"What happened? Oh, Marie-Ange, what were you thinking getting enameled? Your mother will be horrified." Marie-Ange just shook her head.

"Françoise thought it would be pleasing to Her Majesty. But now I do not feel well. I feel faint and my chest hurts." Adelaide pursed her lips and took Marie-Ange's wrist to feel her pulse. She reached into her bag and pulled out one of her oddly-shaped brass and wood devices. It was box-shaped with several metal protuberances that gave it the look of a mechanical insect. It hummed to life at the flick of a switch. She held it to Marie-Ange's chest, the protuberances pressing into the girl's bosom. The pain eased and Marie-Ange took as deep a breath as she could.

"Ah, that feels better."

"It is only temporary, Marie-Ange. You must take care not to overexert yourself."

"I know. I am sorry. I will try harder. Thank you so much."

Adelaide reached over and patted Marie Ange's hand then stood, putting away her medical instrument. She pulled a small bottle of pills out of the bag.

"Take these twice a day. That should help. And please never hesitate to call me if you are feeling unwell." Marie-Ange nodded and tried to smile but her face wouldn't move. She had forgotten the enamel stilling her features.

ꟈ Φ ꟈ

It was past noon when John trudged along the familiar path towards the tradesmen's entrance to the Palace. It had been hours since his encounter with Isabelle but his skin felt charged with sensations and he couldn't get the taste of her mouth out of his mind. What was it about the woman that had made him lose his self-control? John shook off the tempting thoughts and turned to the problem with Henri and how he could possibly help get him out of prison. Perhaps he could speak to the duchesse de Fronsac. Her husband was highly influential in the government, and was rumored to have the ear of President le Scientist.

But what if she took offense at the request? Her influence among the Court ladies was legendary. It was probably her word that had spurred the Queen's commission. He debated making the request back and forth as he entered the Palace and passed through the servants' hall. He was so deep in thought, he barely acknowledged Jeanne as she passed him with an armload of linens.

John passed through the usual crowds of courtiers and factotums on his way to the Queen's suite of rooms. He reached the chequered corridor without being stopped by a guard. There were so many people coming and going, they didn't seem to care. He paced along, close to his destination and still no closer to a decision about asking for a pardon for Henri. Unlike his usual habit, he had not stopped once to admire the decorations or art pieces scattered liberally through the corridors.

He arrived at the entrance to the Queen's suite, two guards at the doors as always. He presented himself and expected to be told to wait. To his surprise, he was ushered in immediately. The soldiers in the Guards' antechamber barely glanced up from their card game as he walked through.

The usher at the door scratched on it with his fingernail, then entered the Queen's audience chamber, John following. The usher inside announced him.

The Queen noticed John and waved him closer. She must be in a good mood today, he thought and hurriedly made his way to her. He bowed deeply, waiting to be spoken to before addressing her.

"Ah, my good painter, you have arrived. I trust you are well. You may begin," she told him. A little surprised at her kind condescension, he replied,

"I thank you for your kind inquiry, Your Majesty." She nodded in response and turned to listen to a comment from one of the ladies-in-waiting. A servant helped John set up his painting supplies and John smiled in thanks.

He turned to look at the Queen, idly glancing around to see if Marie-Ange was present. He didn't spot her at first then froze as he recognized her face, alabaster-white and stiffened under a coat of enamel. She wore a silver grey Court dress with a substantial bustle and train. Her dark brown hair had been powdered to a greyish white.

Oh, Marie-Ange. What have you done?

She was still the most beautiful woman in the room but her halo of youth and vitality was gone. She blended in with the rest of the Court now. Perhaps that was what had pleased the Queen so much. Her young favorite was emulating her look. Seeing the two of them together, they could be mother and daughter, the same painted rosebud mouth and straight aristocratic nose. John surveyed the room full of aristocrats. They all resembled one another. The same nose. The same mouth. He shuddered. The French nobility had been interbreeding for centuries, allowing no outside blood to taint their pure white line. He hadn't realized how similar Marie-Ange was to them until now.

John picked up his palette and a brush and started mixing paint. His hand shook as he stirred. He needed to fall into his art and not think about Marie-Ange's transformation into a Court lady. Taking a deep, shuddering breath, he focused on the painting. John scrutinized his subject, adorned as always in the height of fashion, slim as a girl, and with a perfectly smooth face. The Queen was a mockery of youthful beauty. Pushing aside the thought, he painted steadily, focusing on the lines and colors. He didn't notice the courtiers standing behind him, watching him paint. A quiet voice murmured in his ear.

"Hello, John. What do you think of my new

maquillage?"

It was Marie-Ange. His heart sank. How could he tactfully compliment her without letting his disappointment show? Without taking his eyes from the canvas, he echoed his earlier thought,

"You are the most beautiful woman in the room." She giggled. He let out a soft sigh.

She was so very young.

John stole a look at Marie-Ange as she stood beside him, her eyes on the Queen. Mercoeur, the ever-present Mercoeur, was on her other side, chatting at her. She nodded at his chatter and smiled a faint smile, as much as the enamel would allow.

John wished that Mercoeur would drop off the face of the Earth. He was consuming Marie-Ange's attention. He would probably always do so, having such constant access to her. John felt a yawning chasm between him and his life as a painter and Marie-Ange and her life as a courtier. How could he ever court her properly? He didn't have enough time with her. He thought back to that sweet interlude in the garden, hidden in the tall corridor of hedges. How he wished they were there again. He darted another look at her. She was still standing nearby, facing the Queen with that half-smile on her face.

"How I wish I could kiss you again in the garden," he whispered. She glanced at him quickly then faced forward again. He heard her dress rustle as she shifted in place. She clasped her hands tightly in front of her and let out a little breath.

"Yes. I wish that too. Oh, John, this Court life is so restrictive," she said quietly. He nodded but said nothing, just painted as he was hired to do. There was a burst of tittering laughter from the group of courtiers near Mercoeur and

John heard the Queen say something in response. Mercoeur turned to Marie-Ange and asked her a quiet question. She nodded and he placed her hand on top of his and whirled away with her. They promenaded to another group of courtiers.

The Queen nodded approvingly as the couple moved about together. She said to the surrounding noblewomen in a voice loud enough for John to hear, "I think their families will soon reach an agreement. They make a fine couple, do they not?"

John heard the murmurs of agreement from the courtiers and felt an invisible knife pierce his heart. An agreement between their families. Yes, that was how the nobility arranged marriages, as a contract between the families. The wishes of the young women sold off to the highest bidder to bring money and prestige to their families mattered very little. It was a carefully orchestrated dance, this interbreeding between the noble families, and Marie-Ange would be expected to comply without question.

He wondered how soon they would reach an agreement. She was very young. Surely they didn't mean for her to marry so soon. His chest tightened at the thought of Marie-Ange married to that snake, Mercoeur, subject to his whims, sharing his bed, and bearing his children.

His mind flashed to thoughts of the duchesse de Fronsac and her advances to him. Perhaps when Marie-Ange was a married woman, she would be freer to see him. They could have a discreet affaire. John shuddered, rejecting the idea with disgust. He didn't want a clandestine, immoral affaire. He wanted to make Marie-Ange his wife. But what kind of life could he offer this sheltered and spoilt noblewoman? A house in Montmartre? He didn't have a single servant except for a woman who cooked his dinner and did the heavy cleaning.

Perhaps I can buy a little house with a garden in the country. She would look so sweet in an apron picking apples from a tree.

Mercoeur and Marie-Ange promenaded into view. John glanced at her, clad in yards and yards of silk with her hair piled high into ringlets. This Marie-Ange would not fit in his domestic fantasy. He longed for the sweet young Marie-Ange with her simple chignon and plain white gown. Was she still there, under all that elaborate Court attire? She must be, this was just an aberration, perhaps something forced on her by the older noblewomen in order to make her fit in here. He could change her back into his Marie-Ange. He just needed to get her away from the Court, away from Versailles and away from her arranging family. He couldn't lose her to the artifice of Court life and the arranged marriage with Mercoeur.

Laughter, hard, brittle laughter startled him. His eyes flew towards the group surrounding his love. Was that Marie-Ange laughing? No, it must have been someone else standing near her. Her laughter was sweet, not brittle. Wasn't it?

His shoulders slumped and he opened another jar of paint. More white. He stared down into its milky depths, paralyzed by his misery. He stirred the paint and dabbed at the canvas.

She returned to his side, peeking over his shoulder at the painting. He wanted to hide it from her; he hadn't made much progress. Mercoeur still hovered nearby.

"Does it usually take painters so very long to finish a portrait?" drawled the courtier.

John's back stiffened. "Her Majesty deserves my finest

work and the greatest of care," he said. Mercoeur barked a laugh and moved away. Marie-Ange remained where she was.

"Are you really going to marry that popinjay?" John choked out, his voice rough with emotion. Marie-Ange breathed out softly.

"I suppose. I must do as my family requires."

"Do you? Do you have no choice? Marie-Ange, please, I cannot bear the thought of you married to him." He stole a sideways look at her. Marie-Ange stood upright, rigid in her Court dress. She faced the Queen, showing John only her lovely profile.

"I must do my duty. I was raised to do this. Our union will create a bond between our families and strengthen our bloodlines."

John's mouth twisted in disgust. "You sound like a mare, being bred to make a better racehorse."

She made a little sound of protest but didn't take her eyes off the Queen. "Do not speak so. You make it sound so tawdry. It is my duty to my family and to France."

"Duty. Why do you have to sacrifice yourself on the altar of duty? Let someone else do that."

She shook her head and released another soft, shallow exhalation. "What other option do I have? Marriage to a fellow noble is my lot. I have no useful education. I have been raised to be pretty and pleasing."

John surveyed the room. No-one seemed to be paying attention to the conversation. Even the ever-watchful Queen was listening intently to one of her courtiers.

"You could marry me. You could leave this life of conventions and restrictions and join me in Montmartre." He gave her a quick, pleading look. She gasped quietly.

"Leave Court? I could not possibly do that. It would be

a scandal. My family would disown me. And Her Majesty would be so disappointed in me." John dabbed at the canvas, more to look like he was doing something than to actually add to the painting.

"I see," he said. He was not surprised. He knew she was a dutiful daughter and loyal to the Queen. He had hoped that the strength of her feelings for him would somehow induce her to abandon it all to be with him. How naïve he had been.

"I am sorry, John. I wish I could. If it were just my own feelings to consider, this would be a different matter. I cannot disappoint my family." She swished away slowly into the mass of courtiers.

John struggled to suppress his feelings. His heart felt crushed. He blinked back tears. Pushing Marie-Ange out of his mind, he began to paint ferociously, making progress on the portrait. It was starting to look like the Queen but he still was nagged by the sense of artifice that pervaded the image.

She simply doesn't look human, but perhaps none of the Court portraits look human. Perhaps I am painting beautiful china dolls instead of people. I wonder if that is what Henri meant.

At that thought, he remembered Isabelle's visit. Henri was in prison and needed help. John scanned the room for the duchesse de Fronsac but she wasn't in the Nobles' Salon today. He didn't know who else he could ask for assistance. None of his clients had been as kind to him. They treated him like a tradesman, always requiring him to use the back entrance to the Palace. He gazed at the Queen. He certainly couldn't ask her to release his painter friend from prison after he had seduced her Scientist-doctor. He wondered if she even knew that Adelaide was no longer chaste.

How can I possibly help Henri? I have no power, no influence, despite all my Court clients. What will happen to Henri? I can do nothing.

ꟹ Φ ꟹ

The next day, John sat waiting for the Queen's summons in the same intricately carved hallway that he knew so well from the last five times he'd arrived to paint Her Majesty and been told to wait. Painting the Queen had been so important to his life's goals. He thought if he could penetrate the inner circle at Court as a painter, he would be a success. The Royalist Salon was where he had wanted to display his work. He wasn't interested in the upstarts at the Salon de Paris. It was the traditional, established Salon that he wanted to respect his work. Now here he sat, awaiting Her Majesty's pleasure.

He had painted many ladies of the court. He was the exotic American painter who charmed them as he painted them. He had teased them, actually, titillated them with unspoken promises. He had flattered them and adored their beauty silently, with his eyes. More than one had made subtle advances towards him but he pretended not to notice. Finally, after months of flattering duchesses and comtesses, he had received the summons from the Queen herself.

John had heard rumors about the beautiful Queen of France. He'd seen her portraits but failed to realize how very old those paintings were. He had never been a student of French history so did not know that the woman who had been Queen of France when his mother was a girl was the same Queen now. Seeing her and realizing that the Queen had been Augmented until hardly any of the woman remained had shaken him. He had achieved his goal of being the Court painter for Queen Marie Thérèse, but now he struggled to find any beauty in the mechanical china doll the Scientists had transformed her into.

His goal was split. He had believed he would be able to portray true Beauty and be a renowned painter if he received Court commissions. How was he going to find true Beauty now? His mind settled on Marie-Ange. If only he could paint her. He had sketched her from memory but the sketches never seemed to capture her luminous beauty. He could never quite remember the proportions and lines of her face. He had torn up page after page of failed sketches. He needed her to sit for him, but without her family commissioning him, it was impossible.

Unless he convinced her to sit for him when he was supposed to be painting that wreck, that mechanical queen. Marie-Ange could be his muse.

Yes, that's it. Marie-Ange is the one; she is my pure beauty. I must try to sketch her as well as paint the Queen when I am finally allowed into the Nobles' Salon. If I am ever allowed in.

John had thought ahead and actually eaten a hearty breakfast that morning. He had been faint from hunger the last few sittings when he had been waiting here for hours.

The usher called him in and he walked through the Guards' Room, hoping that Marie-Ange would be present. He tried to hide his grin when he spotted her sitting near the Queen, listening gravely to one of the older ladies. She seemed to be watching him from the corner of her eye. She was lovely as always, luminous despite the enamel on her face. John placed his sketch pad on top of the canvas with his pathetic daubings of the Queen. He started to sketch

Marie-Ange who seemed to be unaware of his drawing.

John was enjoying himself, and felt like he was starting to get a good likeness of Marie-Ange when Mercoeur appeared at his side and exclaimed, "You are commissioned to paint Her Majesty, are you not?"

John started and glowered back at the courtier. Mercoeur was sneering at him. "That is not the Queen." John flushed and said nothing. Mercoeur reached out and snatched the sketch pad off the easel. He stalked over to the Queen and bowed, waiting for a response. The courtiers had all fallen silent, alert to unanticipated drama.

"Yes, Mercoeur? You have something you need to ask of Us?" wheezed the Queen. Mercoeur held up the sketch pad for her to see.

"Your Majesty. This painter is not painting Your glorious Self. He is sketching your lady-in-waiting, Mademoiselle de Laincel." The Queen turned her brilliant blue gaze on John.

"Painter: explain yourself." John bowed towards the Queen.

"Your Majesty. Please forgive me. I was attempting to unlimber my hand before attempting to paint."

"I see. And you thought to draw one of my ladies, rather than myself? That is inappropriate. Unseemly. I no longer wish to have you in My presence. You are dismissed."

John felt the shock of her words to his core.

Dismissed?

"Your Majesty?" he croaked but she ignored him.

Had he lost his commission to paint the Queen? His breath was ragged as he panicked. The servants swooped in to pack up his easel and art case, then removed the table. The usher waited for him to bow to the Queen. They all were looking at him expectantly.

"I most humbly beg your pardon, Your Majesty. I am deeply sorry to have offended you—"

She held up a hand to stop him from continuing. "I do not wish to hear more."

Head bowed, shaking, John left the room, burdened by his equipment and wanting to throw it all away. He had been so close to his ultimate goal. He could have been the Court painter, the greatest painter in France. But it had slipped away. Not only had he lost the Queen's commission, he was likely to get no others from the courtiers. And Marie-Ange. Would he ever get to see her again? Tears welled in his eyes as he contemplated all that he had lost in a moment's indulgence followed by Mercoeur's interference.

Hot anger filled him as he remembered that Mercoeur had caused this. The nobleman with his arrogance and sense of entitlement. He did not deserve Marie-Ange although he certainly seemed to want her. No doubt she would be a suitable wife for him.

But will he love her like I do?

Mercoeur would probably see Marie-Ange as chattel, and not appreciate her beauty. John plodded through the endless hallways of Versailles before finally coming to the servants' hall. Jeanne was there, polishing silver again. A grin crossed her round, brown face when she spotted him but it quickly changed to a look of concern.

"Oh monsieur, are you well? May I get you something? A glass of wine?" John shook his head sadly.

"Ah, sweet little Jeanne. You are so kind to me. I am afraid I must say goodbye to you. I have been dismissed by the Queen so I will no longer be coming to the Palace."

Jeanne gasped then burst into tears. "No, no! How

could that be? You are a great painter, all the ladies say so!" John patted her on the shoulder.

"Goodbye, Jeanne. Be well," he said before exiting the Palace for the final time.

ဢ Φ ဣ

The Nobles' Garden was quiet as John passed through on his way out of Versailles to the train station. There were few courtiers strolling the manicured pathways. Fewer witnesses to his sorrow. The trickling and splashing of water in the fountains was the only sound besides his booted feet tramping on the gravel path.

She dismissed me. Dismissed me with nary a thought and for what?

A little sketch. He went hot and cold at the memory of the Queen's dismissal.

She dismissed me.

The refrain echoed in his head over and over. How could this have happened? His dream had been right there in front of him and now it was gone, snatched away by the capricious Queen. At the thought, John's eyes filled with tears but he sniffed them back. He would not cry. He could not cry. Not here. He strode by the duchesse de Fronsac, barely noticing her as he passed. He neglected his usual obeisance and ignored her look of puzzlement.

He passed through the entrance into the public gardens and was struck by the sudden burst of sounds: people laughing, calling to one another, talking loudly. He cringed at the noise and picked up his speed, hoisting his art case and easel higher on to his shoulder.

"Hey, painter, are ya here to paint me?" screeched a plump woman, stepping in front of him. Her companions howled in laughter. John stopped to avoid crashing into her and eyed her frizzy hair and roughened dark brown skin. He had a sudden longing for Marie-Ange with her smooth tresses and soft white skin. Marie-Ange. His angel. Would he ever see her again?

"Pardon me, *citoyenne*," he muttered, trying to circle around her. She put out a hand to stop him.

"Aww, you won't oblige me with a little sketch? Today is my natal day!" John hesitated. Her companions joined in with cries of support for her idea. Not understanding why, he nodded his assent. The woman's face split in a grin, triumphant in front of her friends. John dropped his equipment to the ground and pulled out his sketchpad and charcoal.

"How do ya want me, m'sieur artist?" The woman asked. John seated her on the edge of a fountain and bade her to sit still. She had obviously been celebrating her birthday with more than one glass of wine and sat giggling on the marble seat. He began sketching, deliberately not thinking, not feeling, just doing. His hand flew across the page and he completed the sketch in what felt like seconds. He studied his drawing. The gentle curve of the woman's cheeks and chin pleased him. He had captured the mischief and the underlying weariness in her eyes. John was startled to discover that he was proud of the work. He dashed his signature at the corner of the page and presented the sketch to the woman with a bow.

"Happy natal day, *madame*."

"*Merci,* monsieur*!* Fancy that! It looks just me!" she said, taking the sketch. She and her friends continued on their way, carrying the sketch like a prize won at a carnival. John watched them go, trying to figure out why he had indulged the woman's request. She was no beauty but she certainly hadn't repelled him like the Queen had. And she had been grateful and simple to please. That was a relief after having to endure the whims of his noble clients.

He continued on his way, feeling drained but somehow calmer.

ꙮ Φ ꙮ

Marie-Ange watched John leave the salon, trying not to cry. She didn't know when she would see him next, now that the Queen had dismissed him. Their worlds were so separate. She had never even been to Montmartre. It was not a proper place for her to visit, too rough and full of uncouth artists and other scoundrels. Sadness washed over her. She bit her lip and tried to draw a deep breath. Curse this stupid corset, she thought as she sat stiffly upright on a stool near the Queen and tried not to fidget.

It was so hot in the crowded Nobles' Salon especially in the extravagant new bustled gown that Marie-Ange wore. She was a little doubtful now about the wisdom of adopting the elaborate Court dress. And the enameling on her face was dreadful. It itched and it made her feel even hotter. She was still not used to stiffness of her face and was sure the enamel would crack at any moment.

The Queen had not said a word to her for hours. She was so tired from sitting there. What was the use of attending the Queen if there *is* nothing to do for her?

"Marie-Ange. Do you know why that painter thought he should sketch you rather than Myself?" The Queen's voice was husky and thin. Marie-Ange started at the sound, having been wrapped up in her own thoughts. She rotated to face the Queen who was watching her intently.

"Your Majesty. I am afraid I am not privy to the

thoughts of Monsieur Saylor," she replied, a quaver in her voice betraying her nervousness. The enamel hid her blush, but somehow the Queen sensed it.

"You seem embarrassed. Nervous, perhaps."

Marie-Ange's eyes dropped down to her lap, hands twisted together. She cleared her throat and, glancing back up, said, "Your Majesty, I am embarrassed at the painter's attention. It is inappropriate."

"Ah, what a very studied response, my dear Marie-Ange. You are quickly becoming a courtier. But my dear, I am very old, you know. I have seen many young ladies arrive at Court and have their heads turned by inappropriate young men. Some of them regain their sense of propriety but others fall into ruin. Which will you be? Are you going to let this painter ruin you?"

Marie-Ange cringed. How could she have guessed? It was eerie how much she seemed to know. "Madame, I assure you that I know my duty."

"Of course you do, Marie-Ange. You are from one of the finest noble families in France. You are also a girl of great feeling and so you may desire to be swept away by love. You may crave romance and excitement after your sheltered life in the country. I must warn you that often leads to disaster. You think me an old woman who remembers nothing of what it is to be young. You are wrong in that regard. I may not still feel those feelings but I watch my young ladies-in-waiting and I see what they are tempted to do. Perhaps you think I do not see clearly? You see, I am removed from the strong passions of the young and can see much more clearly than you."

She stopped talking, wheezing with the effort of her long speech. Marie-Ange swallowed before speaking, her hands sweating inside her gloves.

"Your Majesty, please pardon me if I have upset you. I will do my best to remain apart from those who would lead me astray."

The Queen nodded, the enamel on her face holding her features into its usual semi-melancholic expression that for once felt true to the moment. The whirring and hissing of the Queen's machinery was the only sound coming from the monarch. Marie-Ange was suddenly aware of the Queen's artificiality.

Am I going to end up like her, almost entirely mechanical?

Marie-Ange trembled with horror at the vision, and felt suddenly trapped in her misery. She sat unmoving next to the Queen, the corsetry holding her body still and the enamel on her face restraining even her frown.

ஐ Φ ଓ

Marie-Ange flounced into the duchesse de Fronsac's exquisitely decorated sitting room, her train threatening to tip over a delicate side table. Françoise sipped tea from a blue Japanese china cup and watched her young protégée approach.

"Françoise!" Marie-Ange gasped, hand to her chest. "You must help me. My life, it is ruined. Oh, whatever will I do? I am in despair!" Françoise raised a delicate eyebrow a fraction.

"Ma chère, calm yourself. Please, sit down and have a cup of tea and then we can discuss your ruined life." Marie-Ange flopped into a gilt and wood chair. It creaked alarmingly but Marie-Age didn't notice the sound.

How like Françoise to simply dismiss my anguish. Tea! As if tea could fix this horrible mess that my life has become.

She took the proffered cup with little grace and barely mumbled thanks. Françoise sat quietly as Marie-Ange drank the hot tea before speaking.

"Marie-Ange, you really are in a shockingly bad mood. What has happened?"

Marie-Ange carefully put the delicate cup down on a spindly legged side table. She put a hand back to her chest and sniffed.

"I have received a letter from my Papa. He says, oh, Françoise, he says that he is speaking to the Mercoeurs about marriage. My marriage. He wants me to marry Michel de Mercoeur. Can you imagine a worse fate? I'd rather die!" He voice grew shrill.

"A worse fate. Hmm. I think I can imagine a worse fate but I see that you cannot."

Marie-Ange shook her head, her curls bobbing. "No! It could not be worse. He is a snake. Always slithering around me, hissing his ridiculous compliments in my ear. He is loathsome. I cannot marry him. I just cannot. I cannot marry him because my heart belongs to another."

Françoise reached over and took Marie-Ange's hand. She gazed into the girl's eyes and sighed.

"Have you not learned, ma chère, that our duty is to marry as we are bid. The wishes of our heart are not heard. We are noblewomen of France and we cannot marry for love."

Tears welled up in Marie-Ange's eyes.

"But—no! It is not fair! I cannot stand him. How can I bear it? Françoise, you must help me escape this fate."

Françoise shrugged, sitting back in her chair with a creak of corset bones. "What can I do to help? It is up to your family to arrange your marriage."

"But you can perhaps convince my Papa to look elsewhere for my husband. Or perhaps he could delay this marriage. And in the meantime—" she stopped, afraid to continue. How could she convince Françoise to help her see John?

"In the meantime, you can continue enjoying your little flirtation with the painter?" Marie-Ange drew a quick breath. How did Françoise know about John? Had she seen them together?

"My flirtation? With a painter?" she asked, hoping that Françoise didn't really know anything.

"My dear girl, you cannot fool me. I have seen you watching John Saylor, the man painting the Queen's portrait. He is quite handsome, is he not? And he seems enamored of you. Far below you, of course, but certainly an enjoyable diversion."

"It is not like that!" Marie-Ange burst out. "And he is not painting Her Majesty anymore. Now I do not know when I will ever see him again," she wailed, dabbing her eyes with a scrap of lace.

"He is finished with Her Majesty's portrait? So soon?" Marie-Ange shook her head, eyes downcast.

"He is not finished. The Queen dismissed him."

"Dismissed him? But why?" Françoise leaned forward, looking into Marie-Ange's face. The girl moaned, remembering the look John had given her as he sketched her instead of the Queen.

"He was sketching me instead of painting the Queen and then that sneak Mercoeur pointed it out to the Queen. Oh, I hate him!" Françoise blew out a breath.

"Sketching you? Right in front of the Queen? Well, that was not very clever of him. Her Majesty does notice the little flirtations, you know. And so Mercoeur decided to get him dismissed from the Queen's service. He must have seen your painter as a threat somehow to his suit. Ha! Mercoeur must have been jealous! How delightful."

Marie-Ange cocked her head, trying to figure out why Françoise was pleased by Mercoeur's reaction. Remembering her anguish anew, her head drooped.

"Why should I care if Mercoeur is jealous. He has won. I will never be able to see John if he does not come to Court any more. Oh Françoise, I have nothing left to live for!"

Françoise exhaled an exasperated breath. "Marie-Ange, pull yourself together. I may be able to help you. Leave it to me. I will get your painter back to Court."

Marie-Ange gazed soulfully, eyes wide, at the older woman and nodded. Françoise called for her writing desk. "I will write a letter to Monsieur Saylor telling him to wait a week or so, then return to Court as if nothing had happened. The Queen's memory is poor. She forgets things and she will more than likely forget that she had dismissed him."

Marie-Ange gasped.

"Françoise! You cannot do that! The Queen dismissed him."

The duchesse laughed and lifted one silk-clad shoulder. "I can do it and I will. I cannot wait to see Mercoeur's face when he thinks that the Queen has summoned him back."

Marie-Ange sat back in her seat, staring at this impudent duchesse and wondering about the consequences. She was desperate to see John, but could not shake the fear that something would go very wrong.

Ten

Henri shuffled along a dark hallway, fettered at the wrists and ankles. Two days of interrogation by the Police Secrète had left him exhausted and shaken. He had been unable to tell them anything important. Jean-Luc with his constant circumspection had made sure of that. They were done with him for the time being.

Henri followed a prison warden along a corridor within the dreaded Bastille prison. Henri's legs shook with fatigue as the warden dragged him up yet another set of stone steps. So he wasn't going to be held in one of the octagonal rooms in the mid-levels of the towers? Those, he had heard were reserved for nobility who angered their monarch. They appeared to be headed up, up to the rooms just under the roof that formed the upper story of the Bastille, the *calottes*, he had heard them called. They were exposed to the elements and usually either too hot or too cold for comfort. They reached the top of the stairs and turned into the open passageway. The rain poured in rivulets down the walls. The drops stinging with cold as they hit him in the face.

Eh, but at least I'm not going one of the cachots, those dungeons underground. I don't think they've been used for years, except for holding the poor sods who are recaptured after escaping this place.

It was quiet as they made their way along the upper story. Henri got the impression that few prisoners were occupying the rooms they passed. It was quiet; no snoring or moaning emanated from the cells.

The prison warden led Henri into a room with a stove, basic furniture, curtains and a window; it was shabby and basic rather than uncomfortable. Henri suppressed a snort of ironic laughter.

This cell is a good deal cleaner than my studio flat.

There was a pile of wood next to the stove and since it was chill in the stone room, the warden lit a fire. Henri was surprised at the solicitude. Perhaps things weren't quite as bad as he feared. Perhaps he would be locked up for a few days then released.

"I am most appreciative of your kindness, m'sieur," Henri told his guard as the man removed the shackles from Henri's wrists.

"We are not monsters here at the Bastille, despite what people on the outside may think, m'sieur. It is very late. I am sure you would like to sleep so I will bid you goodnight." Henri, still a little bemused at the kind treatment, said goodnight. The warden closed and locked the door. Hearing the click of the lock reawakened Henri to the fact that he was imprisoned, and in the Bastille. He felt his chest tighten and he eased himself on to a chair in front of the stove.

Warming his hands, he tried not to think about what could happen to him here. He had been arrested for high treason, on the word of Adelaide. She must have a lot of influence for her word to be enough to get a man thrown into prison.

Now what? Would there be a trial? What proof was needed to execute a man for high treason?

He began to shake at the thought.

They used Madame Guillotine to execute traitors to the state. Is that to be my destiny? And what of Isabelle? Will she suffer through association?

Henri's musings became chaotic and muddled and he decided to try to sleep. He stretched out on the creaking bed, and covered himself with an itchy wool blanket. Sleep refused to come. He was probably the latest in a string of prisoners who lay staring at the ceiling, unable to sleep due to worry about their fate. He wondered how many of them were released and how many died here.

Henri, you are being morbid. There is no use in worrying about what could happen.

He needed to get out of here. A prison was no place for an artist. He started to dream about the paintings he was working on and his body relaxed as he imagined finishing the portrait of Isabelle on the divan.

Henri heard a slight scratching at the door then a stealthy jiggling of the lock. He sat up and peered at the door. The sounds continued, until finally he heard a click and the door swung open. Henri waited. A figure stood silhouetted in the dim light from the hallway.

"Desjardins," came a soft voice from the figure. Henri stood up quickly, trying to be as quiet as he could.

"Yes," he whispered. "Who is there?"

"A friend. Come with me. I will help you escape." Henri

did not hesitate. He joined the figure at the door. Henri couldn't make it out but the figure, he thought it was a man, appeared to be dressed in a warden's uniform. The man closed the door and relocked it.

"Better that no-one suspects you are gone for a while." The man ushered him into one of the niches in the hallway and handed him some clothing in a bag. It was another warden's uniform. Henri changed clothes quickly and put his own clothing in the bag. Better not leave anything suspicious around, he thought, then wondered at his sudden talent for subterfuge.

"Now let us go, quickly. Try to look a little more official."

Henri frowned. What did official look like? He must have looked confused because his rescuer explained, "Straighten your shoulders. Don't slouch."

Henri attempted to mimic the man's military posture as they walked side by side. He picked up his feet, trying not to stumble in the poorly light hallways as they made their way down. Probably less expensive to run the prison if they didn't light it when it wasn't necessary.

He realized that he had no idea who the man was nor his motives.

Am I really being rescued or is this a trick? Am I being led to my execution?

His heart was racing at the thought.

"How . . . how are we getting out?" Henri finally blurted out as they approached the ground level.

"The same way I got in. Through the Faubourg St. Antoine gate. Don't worry, the guards are allies. We'll have no trouble there."

"You're part of the Underground," Henri stated. "How

did you know where I was?"

"We have watchers everywhere, just like they have Watchers, only ours see clearly. Hadn't you figured that out yet?" Henri felt a chill at that but remained silent as they paced through the prison. He tried to catch a better look at the man's face but it was shadowed. Who was his rescuer? Henri was on edge and flinched at every shadow, expecting guards to loom out and grab him. After many endless minutes, they reached the Faubourg St. Antoine gate.

This was the moment of truth. Would the guards seize him and throw him back into his room? Was this is a trick to make him vanish? They could throw him into the moat. There appeared to be water in it. It was dark and murky. He would drown and no one would know.

Henri and his unknown rescuer approached the guards. The guards nodded to them. The drawbridge was down and their footsteps echoed on the wood slats as they crossed it. Within moments, they were outside the prison and in the street. Henri took a long, shuddering breath. He was out. He had been rescued from the Bastille. As they approached a corner, a steam carriage came puttering up. The driver waved them over.

"Ah good, you have managed to escape. I did not think there would be trouble. We have the many allies within the walls of the Bastille. Now we go quickly. I will you take to a safe house."

Henri recognized the cadence of the man's odd French as he spoke. It was Jean-Luc. They climbed in and the steam carriage rolled away, hissing and rattling along the dark streets.

ꟿ Φ ꟿ

Arthur arrived promptly at nine in the morning for his breakfast date with John. He was impeccably attired in a dark navy suit. How very like him to be so prompt, John thought.

"Good morning, my friend," John greeted him. They shook hands, eschewing the Parisian cheek kiss. John had brewed the coffee himself although his cook had prepared the food. He was particular about his coffee. He ground the beans each morning before brewing the pot on the little gas burner on the sideboard. John watched Arthur survey the comfortable dining room furnished with a solid wooden sideboard and table. The wooden floor was polished to a warm russet brown. The room was just the right size for a cozy meal.

"It was so kind of you, John, to ask me to breakfast and ah—is that coffee? It smells delicious."

"I always make my own coffee. It is so much better that way. Let me pour you a cup." They sat down at the table, cups of steaming coffee in their hands. John lifted the dish covers to reveal a cooked American-style breakfast of eggs and ham steaks. There were even bowls of grits, fluffy biscuits and a bowl of sausage gravy. At the sight of the food, Arthur cried out and clapped his hands.

"John! This is a treat! How did you manage a proper American breakfast? I have already grown weary of weak milky coffee and pastries for breakfast. I need more substantial fare to start my day." John nodded. He had hoped to surprise his friend with a taste of home.

"My cook grumbled but I convinced her with the promise of an extra half day off. I do not eat this well every day." With little conversation, the two men devoured their meal.

John mixed butter into his grits and became transfixed by the melting, swirling butter.

"Do you always examine your food so thoroughly?" Arthur asked. John glanced up and shrugged.

"I apologize. I'm a little preoccupied today."

"Oh? Is something wrong?" John groaned. The loss of the Queen's commission weighed heavily on him but he was reluctant to admit his failure. Arthur was scrutinizing him, his eyebrows questioning, a kindly smile on his face. Worry over Henri and shame over his dismissal overwhelmed him and his need to speak overwhelmed him. He drew in a heavy breath. The doorbell jangled discordantly, interrupting John before he could speak. His forehead creased.

Who on Earth could that be? It's far too early for any of my worthless Parisian acquaintances to be out visiting.

"Please excuse me, I will go and see who that is," he said before heading down the stairs to his front door. He opened the heavy oak door, a frown twisting his mouth, and discovered Henri on his doorstep. Henri's shoulders were hunched and he was looking around furtively.

"Henri, what on Earth are you doing here? Quickly, come inside." John dragged him over the threshold, scanning the street as he did, and closed the door. He took a closer look at Henri. The man was shivering, wearing just shirtsleeves, and his eyes were bloodshot and wild.

"John, I need your help," Henri said simply.

"Good morning to you, Henri! There is plenty of breakfast left," Arthur called. He was standing at the top of the stairs. John and Henri exchanged looks. They definitely needed to talk. The last John had heard Henri was in the Bastille. How did he get here? And why was he out so early in the morning? This was most certainly a mystery that needed solving.

"Come upstairs and have something to eat. Then we can talk about whatever it is you need." Henri nodded and followed John up the stairs. He smiled faintly at Arthur and the men exchanged quiet greetings. John took another plate for Henri out of the sideboard and poured him a cup of coffee. Henri accepted it, sipping the hot liquid with obvious satisfaction. He was still shivering so John got up and put more wood on the fire.

"Have something to eat," John invited. Henri surveyed the food carefully, then pulled a face.

"What is this?" he asked. "Have you no croissants or rolls?" Arthur laughed, a short high bark of a laugh.

"This is a proper American breakfast; it will warm you up. I do not know how you Parisians can live on the insubstantial bits you call breakfast." Henri raised an eyebrow. He patted his substantial torso and replied,

"I do not appear to be suffering for my Parisian diet. Hmpf. Perhaps I will try one of these fluffy roll things. Pass the butter, please."

Henri chomped his biscuit, slurped his coffee then sat back and released a long, slow breath, his posture relaxed.

"Henri, what is going on? Isabelle was here yesterday morning and she was very upset. She told me she wanted my help. But now here you are."

Henri tensed up again and, throwing a glance at Arthur, replied, "A friend helped me leave . . . that place. He took me to . . . somewhere safer."

John was confused. Who was this mysterious friend? Was Henri claiming to have actually escaped the Bastille? John wanted to ask for more details but Henri obviously did not want to talk freely in front of Arthur.

"Perhaps I should take my leave so that you two can continue your discussion privately," Arthur offered, his mouth turned down. John suppressed a smile.

He looks so offended, like a chicken disturbed from its nest.

"That depends. Have you made a decision, Arthur?" Henri asked. John was baffled and gawked from one man to the other.

Decision? What is going on between them?

Arthur nodded slowly, mouth pursed.

"About your Naturalist revolution? Henri, you know I am sympathetic to your cause but . . . it is just too dangerous for me. I am here by the grace of the French government. If I allow myself to become embroiled in this movement, I could be caught and sent back to the United States." He stopped, eyes distant. "I can't go back there. I'm sorry but I can't join you." He dropped his gaze to the ground.

Henri's face sank with dismay. "Oh. I see. That disappoints me, mon ami. I was hoping you would join me." The men stood, not looking at each other, an awkward silence between them. Arthur raised his head and sniffed.

"Shall I leave so that you may share your news with John?"

ജ Φ ଓ

Henri scrutinized Arthur, trying to decide whether he could be trusted. Before his encounter with the Police Secrète, he wouldn't have given it a second thought. He sensed innate nobility in Arthur that would not allow him to betray Henri, even if they were not fighting together in a revolution. He breathed deeply before responding.

"Please, stay. I will tell you my tale. It is one of surprise, adventure, fear. I have been inside the dreaded Bastille as a prisoner but I miraculously escaped its clutches with the help of my friends, who are of the same philosophy as I. It appears we have many allies throughout France; allies who would not see me remain imprisoned. But alas, now I am a fugitive from the law. I cannot remain in Paris, or even in my beloved France. I must flee; I must leave as soon as I can." John's face fell.

"Oh, no, mon frère. You have to leave France? But why? You love your country. You will be an exile."

Henri nodded, mouth drooping, eyes grave. He hated the idea of running away, leaving his home but he knew his life was forfeit if he remained. His escape from the Bastille had turned him into a fugitive. He didn't want to be recaptured and imprisoned in the bowels of that prison.

"Until France is free from the shackles of her mechanical rulers, it is not safe for me to be here. My heart may break but I must leave my beloved France. I can no longer aid in restoring our human monarch, at least not here. I must pass the mantle to another. John, you have never committed to the Naturalists but I know you must be sympathetic." John reached out and grasped Henri's shoulder but didn't say anything.

Arthur said, "You said that you cannot be in France while her current rulers are in power. You mean to somehow depose these mechanical monarchs?"

Henri nodded.

"Those I have spoken to in the Underground believe that if the Queen is, uh, decommissioned, the true monarch, the duc d'Orléans , will be able to enter France and take control. They feel that the King may not even be alive and that there is a pretense going on to keep the power at Versailles with the Queen."

Arthur looked puzzled. "Decommissioned? Whatever do you mean by decommissioning the Queen?"

Henri watched John who sat drinking his coffee slowly. John's shoulders slumped as he sighed his response. "The Queen appears to be mostly machine, not really a human anymore."

Arthur's eyes opened wide and his mouth dropped open. He gasped, "A machine? So then France is truly being ruled by the Scientists and their creations? That is an abomination. Decommissioned? Do you mean there is a way to shut down this mechanical thing?"

Henri shifted uncomfortably in his chair. He had never seen the Queen and only had John's word for the extent of the Queen's Augmentation. In fact, the whole of the Underground's new strategy hinged on John's testimony. But the Scientists who had joined the Underground assured Henri that if the Queen was at least partially powered by the new electric motors, she could be shut down with a stun bomb. The problem would be getting close enough to her for it to work. That was where John's assistance was required.

"Henri," John spoke quietly, interrupting his thoughts. "The Underground wishes to . . . shut down the Queen? Permanently? Would that not be murder?" Henri's chest tightened. He shifted in his chair. He hadn't really considered it that way.

"I thought you said she was a machine, not a person," Henri retorted. John was silent for a moment before he replied.

"It seems that way, although there is something of the person still there. It is as if her consciousness is trapped in a mechanical form."

Arthur shuddered. "It is cruel to do that to someone.

Unnatural. Surely she cannot want to remain that way? And how long has she been trapped in this machine? You said she is very old. She could have been existing as a machine for decades."

"I think it has been a gradual process of replacing her human organs and limbs as they failed with age. She has a Scientist-doctor in constant attendance to keep her alive." At John's mention of Adelaide, Henri flinched. She was responsible for his coming exile. He wanted to hate her. Would this decommission of the cyborg Queen be some sort of revenge? Is that what he wanted, to take away Adelaide's life as she had taken away his? Or was this truly the way to restore France to the people? He stared down at the dregs of his coffee.

"It is time for her to be allowed to pass from this life," Arthur said, face determined. "Someone must shut down the machine keeping her in this state of quasi-life and let her go into the arms of God."

"John, you are the only one of us who can get close to her," Henri noted. He and Arthur watched John, eyebrows raised. John lowered his eyes and with a flush across his cheekbones, said in a low voice, "I cannot help you, mon frère. I have been dismissed from the Queen's service."

ꝏ Φ ꝏ

John braced himself for his friends' reactions. Henri gasped, his jaw dropping in astonishment. Arthur merely frowned.

How typical of them.

"What? What happened? Did you violate some rule of protocol?" Henri asked.

John glanced up then dropped his eyes down again. He

rubbed his forehead, struggling for composure. He drew in a shaky breath before facing them again.

"I was not doing what I was there for."

Henri cocked his head to the side and asked, "What *were* you doing?"

John's reply was so low that the other two had to lean close to hear.

"I was sketching Marie-Ange."

Henri burst out laughing. John glowered at his brother as the man added salt to John's wounds. "You were dismissed because you would sketch the lovely young Marie-Ange rather than the Queen? Oh John, you have lost your senses."

"Or my heart," John said, his inner eye filled with Marie-Ange's lovely face.

Arthur *tsked.* "Then you are destined to truly lose your heart, my friend. Even I know that French nobles do not marry American painters."

Henri guffawed, slapping his knee. "Who said anything about marriage? He should wait until the delightful Marie-Ange is married to some other noble. Then he can have a dalliance with her."

Arthur shook his head, eyes wide open. "Henri! Please do not advise John to an amoral path to love—"

John's anger flared, burning away his uncertainty and melancholy. "Henri, that is enough! Enough, do you hear me?" His voice rose almost to a shout. "Don't you understand? I love her. She means so much more to me than someone to warm my bed. I would spend the rest of my life with her if I could. I will not stand here and listen to you sully that with your lewd banter. Ah, but it no longer matters," John said, suddenly deflated. He dropped his head into his hand. "Without access to the Court, I have no way of seeing her. The nobles will not hire me now that the Queen has expressed her disapproval of me. My career is over and I have lost Marie-Ange." The three men sat in silence. John got up and went to the sideboard. He systematically went through the motions to make more coffee.

"More coffee, *mes amis*?" He offered the fresh pot to the others after pouring himself another cup.

The men sat silently. As they relaxed into drinking their coffee, they heard a knock at John's front door. Henri started, spilling his coffee.

"The Police Secrète! They have found me! I must leave." He jumped up and searched for an escape route, his head swinging back and forth wildly. John stood and beckoned to him.

"Come, you can leave through the kitchen." They all hurried into the hallway and down the stairs. Henri dashed to the back of the house. John watched until he was out of view before opening the door. It was a liveried servant from Versailles. John exhaled with relief that the unexpected visitor was not a policeman.

"How may I help you?" John asked. The servant bowed and handed him a letter.

"A letter for Monsieur John Saylor. Are you him?" John nodded and thanked the man, handing him a few coins. The servant bowed again and turned to go. John shut the door and relaxed against it. He smiled at Arthur, his mouth crooked with relief.

"Henri! There is nothing to worry about! It was a servant from Versailles," John called down the hall. Henri's shaggy head poked out from behind the kitchen door.

"It wasn't the Police Secrète? Oh la, I thought for certain I was captured!" The three men laughed softly with relief and headed back up to John's parlor. They resumed their seats and took up their coffee cups again. Henri refilled his spilled coffee. He spotted the letter in John's hand.

"You received a letter from Versailles? Open it, John! Let us hear what they have to tell you," he said. John's face fell, remembering the missive in his hand.

"It is probably an official letter of dismissal from the Queen. Here, you read it." He handed it to Henri who tore open the envelope with no regard for the expensive stationary. Henri sniffed the fragrant paper appreciatively.

"Someone likes you, judging by the perfume," he said. He perused the contents of the note and raised his shaggy eyebrows up high, then laughed. John and Arthur frowned at his unexpected response.

"What does it say? Come now, Henri, do not keep us in suspense," begged Arthur. Henri waved the note in the air.

"It is from the duchesse de Fronsac. One of your clients, I assume?" Henri asked, quirking an eyebrow at John who nodded in assent. "She says that you are to simply return to Court as if nothing has happened. She believes that the Queen's memory is poor and she will not remember that she dismissed you after a few days."

John gave a short bark of laughter and shook his head. "Let me see that letter. That sounds preposterous." John silently read the letter to himself, a frown creasing his forehead.

Henri sipped his coffee and said, "If you do have *entrée* once again to the Queen's presence, you *can* help me free France from the mechanical tyranny."

"And allow Henri to remain in his homeland," Arthur reminded John.

"If I have entrée. What if La Duchesse is wrong? What if I am barred from admittance?"

Henri shrugged and said, "Then you simply leave the

Palace and we try something different."

John rubbed his face, lost in thought. "Arthur. Henri. How do I know this is the right thing to do? How will getting rid of the Queen affect those who are really in power? Will it change anything?"

Henri placed a hand on John's shoulder and squeezed.

"You mean the Presidente le Scientist? He will be ousted, with the rest of his cronies. And France will return to her natural state, without its mechanical rulers. A France with proper weather and without those horrible clanking soldiers. It all hinges on you, mon frère." Henri smiled.

"If the Queen is removed," Arthur said, "you would have a bloodless revolution, my friend. Do you not agree that this would be preferable to all the lives lost for our own revolution?" Arthur's tone was earnest, pleading almost. Henri's expression echoed his words. They both waited for John's response.

"Before I agree, I must know what it is you require of me."

Henri shrugged. "You will be in no danger, I'm sure. My contact will arrange everything. You just need to get into the Palace." John searched Henri's familiar face for reassurance. If for no other reason, John wanted to assure that his brother could live safely here in his homeland.

"Very well. I will do this thing." Henri whooped in triumph and patted him on the back, hard. Henri's face glowed with exultation. "What will I be required to do, Henri?"

"Not to worry, mon frère. The men of the Revolution will make all the arrangements."

ഌ Φ ಌ

His art case weighed heavily on his shoulder as John boarded the train to Versailles. He hadn't examined the small stun device Jean-Luc had placed in the case but it was so heavy, it must be solid metal. John pushed the thought out of his head. If he thought too much about what he was about to do, he would not be able to go through with it.

The train whistle blew close to him and he started, gasping. I must try to stay calm, he told himself. His hands were sweating. He tried to rub them dry on his trousers as he searched for a seat on the train. It was half-empty since most holiday makers to Versailles had already left Paris. He slipped into a seat in an empty compartment and exhaled a sigh of relief. He didn't want to make idle conversation. He was too wound up for that.

Out the window, he spotted a troop of the Police Secrète in their distinctive dark gray uniforms on the platform next to the train. His heart started pounding. What were they looking for? He was frozen, transfixed to the sight of the policemen walking down the platform. They appeared to be questioning people at random.

He stole another glance out the window. The gray-clad officers were right outside, at the door into the train car where John sat. His guts felt as if they had turned to hot liquid, and he couldn't catch his breath, couldn't move. Were they boarding the train? John peeked again. No, they were talking to a fawn-colored man in a shabby suit. All of a sudden, two of them grabbed the man's arms and they all marched off, dragging the struggling man along with them.

John drew in a shuddering breath. They hadn't discovered him carrying a bomb but instead, they had dragged off that man for what? Suspicious behavior?

I need to calm down and look . . . normal? Unsuspicious? I don't want to end up like that poor wretch. What if they were to catch me with this case? It has my name on it.

He glanced around to make sure no-one was watching and quickly pulled his art case onto his lap. He tried to pry the nameplate off it. It was screwed on tightly. He flicked open the case and pulled out a small knife. It seemed to work fairly well as a substitute screwdriver and after a few minutes, he managed to get the little brass plate off the art case. He tucked the plate into his pocket and replaced the art case in a cubby under the seat.

His stomach felt sour from the rush of nerves he had experienced when he thought the Police Secrète were going to arrest him. This escapade again seemed like a very bad idea, foolhardy, reckless, not at all like him. How had he let Henri convince him to do this? As he sat trying to decide whether he should just abandon this foolish venture, the train jerked into motion.

"Damn," he swore under his breath. Now he was committed to head to Versailles. He could turn right around and come back to Paris but the device was set to engage five hours after the Underground operative had handed it to him. John had no idea how to switch it off, or if that was even possible. He pulled out his pocket watch. He had four and a half hours before it would engage, disrupting any electric-powered devices in a fifty meter radius. The Underground man had assured him that it would be completely harmless to nonAugmented humans such as himself.

John had neglected to ask what would happen to the art case. Would it too be destroyed or would it remain intact? He had removed the identifying nameplate but how many art cases did people leave sitting around Versailles? Would he be under suspicion? John shook himself mentally. No doubt the art case would be destroyed. The Underground surely would not risk him being implicated in the Queen's assassination. He hoped. He shifted on the seat, his wool trousers itching. He scratched his leg and tugged on the offending fabric. He was carrying a stun bomb into the Palace of Versailles but had no idea how it worked. Would it affect the electric lights? What about the Augmented guards? Would they be damaged too? That would make getting out a little easier, wouldn't it?

The bustling streets and towering buildings of Paris passed by quickly, too quickly for John's comfort. Soon they were in the countryside. He sat alone in the train compartment, watching the scenery dully, without his usual delight in its aesthetic qualities. The trees were changing color and their senescent shades flashed by. Soon the leaves would fall and the bleakness of winter would take over the landscape.

John hoped that he would be here to see the season change and not imprisoned in the hulking fortress of the Bastille when winter came.

Henri had brought men from the Underground to his house, hooded, ominous figures. They had all assured him that there was no risk; he was to simply leave the art case in the Nobles' Salon and depart. No one would pay attention to him. But what if they were wrong? He glanced at his pocket watch again. Four hours until this device engaged. What if the guards kept him waiting in the corridor as before? He drummed his fingers on his knee and tapped his foot. He wished that Marie-Ange would be there. This would most likely be the last time he would see her. He had to give up his unrealistic dreams of loving her. She had already refused to leave Court to be with him. This would be his goodbye to her and in all likelihood, to his life as a Court painter. Who knew what would happen to the Court without their Queen? Would the *Duc d'Orleans* reassemble them into a Court once more or would he gather his own favorites? John groaned. He would have to establish his reputation anew. Suddenly weary, he laid his head back against the seat and closed his eyes.

The door rattled open. John jumped, his heart racing. It was the conductor, collecting tickets.

“We will be arriving at Versailles in a few minutes, m'sieur,” he said. Was he looking suspiciously at John's art case? Could he be an undercover agent for the Police Secrète? John mumbled something in return, wishing the conductor would leave. Fortunately, he did not seem inclined to stay and chat, discouraged by John's lack of conversation. He nodded and moved on to the next compartment. John's heart was still pounding and the view of the village of Versailles did nothing to help settle his agitation. He reached down with trembling hands to remove his art case from under his seat.

John restrained the urge to open the case and check that the device remained hidden. He had watched the operative place the small, undistinguished wooden box underneath a tray of paints. John shouldn't need to reveal the box to actually do any painting. Chances of its discovery were low.

The train shuddered to a halt, clanking and hissing. They had arrived. John stood, clutching the art case to his chest. He would be at the Palace shortly. He hoped his courage would not fail him.

ꟾ Φ ꟾ

The great gilt doorway leading into the Queen's suite of rooms loomed in front of him, flanked by hard-eyed guards. He was here. It was the moment of truth. Would the duchesse be correct? Would they indeed let him pass into the Nobles' Salon? He approached the guards, his mouth suddenly full of bile. He swallowed hard.

"Bonjour. I am Monsieur Saylor, here to paint Her Majesty," he told the guards. They gazed at him without expression. John tried to smile but his face felt stiff, unyielding, like that of his enameled clients.

After a pause, one of the guards said, "Her Majesty may not be receiving today."

John surveyed the corridor around him. He had failed to notice that the usual crowd of petitioners was missing. His heart sank. Not receiving? How could she not be receiving, today, of all days. John stared at the guard, waiting. The guard finally sighed, reached behind him, and tapped the door. A few moments went by, endless moments. John tried to catch his breath but could only take short, shallow breaths. The door opened and an usher stepped through. He looked up and down at John, apparently not recognizing him.

"Her Majesty is not accepting petitions today," he declared.

"Pardon, m'sieur but I am not a petitioner. I have come to paint Her Majesty's portrait," John replied. Would the usher know that the Queen had dismissed him? John held his breath. Please let him not know. The usher frowned.

"I was not told to expect a painter," he said. John thought quickly.

"I have been to paint Her Majesty several times in the past few weeks. Perhaps no-one thought it noteworthy enough to trouble you with," he said. The usher shrugged.

"Ah, that may be. This may not be an appropriate time for a painter to be admitted. Please wait." John felt his heart squeeze tight. He had trusted that he would be whisked inside as he had been the last time he was here. He shifted the art case from one hand to another. It was so very heavy. The guards paid him no attention. He moved over to the wall and placed the art case on the floor before rubbing his hands to relieve the soreness from carrying the heavy case.

How long would he have to wait this time? He pulled out his pocket watch. Two and a half hours before the device would engage. Henri had promised a diversion to allow John to escape unnoticed. When would the diversion happen? Would it be another explosion?

He tried to calculate how many meters he was from the Queen. Depending on where she was in the Nobles' Salon, he thought she was within range of the device. He could just walk away, leaving the case where it was. But what if someone discovered it and moved it? Glancing to his side, he noticed a pedestal with a bust mounted on it. He could slide the case behind the pedestal, out of sight. Keeping an eye on the guards, he used his foot to slide the case on the polished floor to a spot half hidden behind the pedestal. Casually, he moved closer to the pedestal, pretending to examine the bust. He slid the case further behind the pedestal, then stepped back, as if to admire the sculpture from a different vantage point. He couldn't see the case anymore. Good. He could just leave now and hope that the device would reach.

The door to the Queen's suite clicked open behind him and a voice called,

"Monsieur Saylor. Her Majesty is ready for you." John rotated to face the usher, smiling weakly.

"Of course." He quickly reached back and retrieved his art case, hoping the usher and guards hadn't noticed that it was hidden. He started towards the doorway. No more delays. He was carrying a bomb into the Queen's suites that would kill her in less than two hours. He was about to become a regicide. His legs shook as he walked. His breath came in gasps that he tried to hide.

"Wait, m'sieur, your case must be searched before you can enter," a guard demanded. John froze.

Searched? Since when did they search my case?

The guard reached for the art case. John's fingers were slick with sweat and the handle slipped out of his grip. The guard took it from him and placed it on the ground. Barely breathing, John watched the guard open up the case and poke around at the brushes and paint tubes. The detritus of an artist's tools hid the little wooden box containing the bomb, but if the guard started removing items, he would see it. The usher huffed, obviously not accustomed to waiting. The guard shrugged, closed and latched the case, and handed it back to John.

That was pure blind luck. I was sure he'd find the device.

John and the usher stepped through into the Guards' Room, full of a dozen or more guards. John tried to remember if there were always that many. He wasn't sure. He'd never paid attention to them. Of course, he'd never had anything to hide like a bomb that would go off and kill their Queen.

John wondered again about the guards. The device would disrupt the soldier's Augmentations. But would it kill them? That would make him responsible for killing Her Majesty's guards as well as the monarch herself. And what of her courtiers? How many of them were Augmented? He remembered the older woman he had tripped on his first visit. She was Augmented. If she was present, the device would knock her over and probably kill her too. How many people would he be killing today? It was hard to tell under the layers of fabric and cosmetics how many of them were Augmented with mechanical hearts or limbs. John rarely even looked at them. Except for Marie-Ange. His natural beauty who had succumbed to the lures of Court, adopting their enamel and elaborate toilettes.

John nearly stumbled into the usher as they reached the closed door of the Nobles' Salon. The usher reached up with his little fingernail and gently scratched the door. John peeked back at the guards. They were watching him. Did they always watch him?

The door opened and John was finally in the Nobles' Salon. A sudden thought occurred to him. Was Mercoeur here? Would he remind the Queen that she had indeed dismissed him? John had not considered that possibility. He cast his gaze about wildly but spotted only court ladies. The usher led him forward, John's burden banging against his thigh. Then she was there in front of him, the Queen. The whirring noise was louder and somewhat irregular today. She examined him as he approached. Would she remember? John bowed deeply.

"Painter. I see you have returned," was all she said. The duchesse had been right. The Queen had forgotten that she had dismissed him. More incredible luck. John quickly set up his supplies, not looking around for Marie-Ange or the duchesse. He did not want to be distracted now. Anyone bothering to check had to be convinced that he was painting the Queen in earnest. He noticed his hand trembling as he mixed his paints. He took a deep steadying breath and looked up at the Queen. Marie-Ange was standing nearby, whispering to the duchesse de Fronsac. She didn't spare him a glance.

Was she being discreet? Or had she forgotten him already?

He looked back quickly at his canvas, not wanting the Queen to notice that his gaze had strayed from her. For once, she was sitting quietly, posing for him. Her ladies chattered to her but she seemed to ignore them, not responding with her usual vivacity. John wondered if she felt ill. Or was she malfunctioning? Could she feel ill? Could she feel anything?

John painted slowly, his hand shaking. He glanced down at his open art case. The little wooden box containing the stun device remained hidden from view. Would it make noise when it engaged? He wished he had thought to ask what damage it would do to the case, if anything. He put down his brush to check the time. Less than an hour. The Queen noticed him looking at his watch.

"Have you another engagement, m'sieur?" John glanced up in surprise.

"I beg your pardon, Your Majesty?" he asked. Her glowing eyes were fixed on his and he couldn't look away, although he knew it was against protocol to hold her gaze.

"You checked your watch. I wondered if you have somewhere else you wish to be besides here in My presence," she said, her voice slow and rasping. John shook his head and bowed in her direction.

"No, Your Majesty, I have nowhere else I wish to be," he said. Seeming to be satisfied, she nodded her head and motioned for him to continue. He picked up his brush again but stood still. He felt as if his hand was wooden, unable to bend or move. He needed to leave. He couldn't stay here any longer but he couldn't figure out a way to leave the art case without someone noticing. He dabbed at the canvas, then winced as he realized that he had painted white over the burgundy of the Queen's gown.

Time was running out. Would he have to remain here when the bomb went off? Would there be enough chaos for him to be able to escape? What had happened to the diversion the Underground had planned?

"John," Marie-Ange's voice was quiet and close by. He jumped, and a warmth spread through his body at her proximity. She and the duchesse had moved to stand behind him and were pretending to talk to each other. Marie-Ange was holding an ornate Japanese fan in front of her face and was fanning herself slowly.

"Marie-Ange," John murmured. "Was my return here inspired by you?"

She laughed softly. "Yes, I recruited the duchesse de Fronsac to assist me," she said. At the word *recruit*, John went cold again, remembering why he was here. He needed to leave soon.

"Marie-Ange, I still want you to leave with me. We could be so happy together," he said.

"Oh, John, I wish I could," she replied, sadness tinging her faint voice. He knew that would be her answer. She was loyal to the Queen, loyal to her class. She would not disappoint her family by leaving this life and marrying a portrait painter, no matter how respectable he might be.

The Queen was still posing, sitting so still he wondered if she had ceased to function. He strained to hear the whirring of her motors, over the chatter. It was still there. He wondered when the Royal Winder had last wound her clockwork battery. Perhaps she was winding down. If the device did as intended, she would never need to be wound again.

Assassin. Regicide.

I could leave now, take the art case with me and the device would go off away from her and I wouldn't kill her. I don't have to do this. I can leave before the device kills her.

He started to pack up his supplies. He had clicked the latch on the case when he heard a muffled boom and the electric chandeliers shook wildly, flickering on and off. Some of the women screamed and guards came running into the room. Some of the courtiers rushed over to the Queen to check on her while others ran out of the room through various doors.

John glanced around and saw that no one was watching him. He took advantage of the chaos and slipped out of the room. As he passed a pair of guards, he overheard one say, "It must have been another bomb. Despite all these extra checks, the Underground has infiltrated the Palace again."

Eleven

Adelaide stumbled around in her dark laboratory. Why had the lights gone out? She hit her knee against a piece of equipment and cried out in pain. Slowing her progress to the windows, she picked her way around the clutter, not wanting to break something or hurt herself again. She pulled back the curtains a little, just enough to let some light in. Adelaide peered out into the courtyard and saw soldiers rushing by outside. What was going on? Had the terrorists attacked Versailles with another bomb? At least her laboratory had been unscathed this time.

She gazed back at the Automated Dauphin, lying on the worktable, safe from the saboteurs now. Zoé's destruction of the arterial connector had delayed progress on it considerably. Adelaide still couldn't fathom how after working so closely together, she had missed the fact that Zoé was a traitor, loyal to the Naturalist cause rather than the Scientist caste. As she thought about it, she remembered little things that had delayed the completion of the automaton, little mistakes that Zoé had made.

At the time, the mistakes had seemed innocent, purely accidental. Now she knew that Zoé had been sabotaging the project all along. Adelaide shook her head. She had been such an idiot. Now her eyes had been opened in more than one way. With that, images of Henri, laughing and teasing, filled her mind. She had been told that Henri had escaped the Bastille, rescued presumably by members of the Naturalist Underground.

Zoé had not been so lucky.

News of her execution had reached Adelaide earlier that day. Such a shame. Zoé could have had a solid career as a Scientist, respected and earning far more than others in her family. Without an assistant, she wasn't sure how she would be able to finish the Automated Dauphin before the King and Queen were unable to function, before their ancient human brains gave out. The Queen already showed signs of dementia and memory loss. It would be only a matter of time before she too became catatonic like the King. Without even a semi-public figurehead, the Scientists would have a hard time keeping the duc d'Orléans out of France and off the throne.

She put her hand to the glass, feeling its smooth coldness under her fingers. The people of France still suffered from the cold of winter and were more likely to revolt then. Adelaide felt a churning in her belly at the thought.

ஐ Φ ঙ

John's shoes clattered on the parquet floor outside the Queen's Rooms. People rushed back and forth, paying no attention to him. He stepped into a side hallway, heading for the tradesmen's entrance. Reaching into his pocket, he pulled out his watch.

Fifteen minutes.

John walked briskly through the seemingly endless corridors. He didn't run. He didn't want to draw attention to himself. He dodged down a hallway to avoid a troop of soldiers, moving away from the shouts of frantic courtiers. He stepped around a corner, walking fast. John heard a cry and, darting a quick glance behind him, turned into yet another corridor. He stopped, seeing a completely unfamiliar hallway and realized that he was lost.

I must have taken a wrong turn somewhere. Or several wrong turns.

He tried to retrace his steps and found a vaguely familiar chequered marble corridor. No one was in the corridor as he followed it along, hoping to find the way out. From ahead of him, he heard clicking footsteps. Someone in high heels was approaching. He turned a corner and saw Marie-Ange headed in his direction. They spotted each other simultaneously.

"John!" she panted, out of breath. Aghast, John realized that she was carrying his art case. "Why did you leave so suddenly? Were you afraid? You forgot your art case in all the confusion!" He reached out to take the heavy case from her, hands trembling. He gazed into her shining brown eyes.

"Marie-Ange. What are you doing here? Why did you follow me?" he replied, deliberately not answering her questions. What was she thinking, chasing him through the hallways of Versailles? Had someone followed her out of the Queen's Rooms? Marie-Ange put her hand to her chest, trying to catch her breath. Her hand was pale and bloodless.

"I am coming with you, John. I cannot be happy here, forced into a loveless marriage with that snake Mercoeur, forced to sit meekly beside the Queen. I feel suffocated." She reached up to her enameled face as if to remove the cosmetic. "I am leaving Court. To be with you," she said, smiling up at him. Her face was luminous, happy. John hardly knew what to think. She was leaving Court? Who knew that she had left? Marie-Ange had the art case, which meant that the Queen was still alive. Or had the device already engaged?

Marie-Ange's face changed. She must have noticed that he was not smiling in return. "Did you not want me to leave with you after all? Were you just toying with me?" John started towards her, his hand outstretched.

"No, my love . . .," he started to say then a low whine rose from the art case in John's arms. An intensely loud bang erupted from the case, splintering the wood and knocking John and Marie-Ange backwards onto the floor. The air rushed out of John's lungs as his head cracked against the marble floor. Paint brushes and tubes showered over their prone bodies. Waves of dizziness and nausea washed over John. He blinked and gasped for air. Struggling up to his elbows, he could see Marie-Ange lying flat on her back on the floor, motionless.

"Marie-Ange?" He couldn't hear his own voice but felt his mouth move. "Marie-Ange!" There was no response. He sat up, his head spinning. Fighting down the nausea, he slowly crawled across the marble floor to her side.

She lay unmoving in a pile of fabric and boning. He pulled her to him and softly slapped her cheeks. She didn't respond. He slapped a little harder and shook her, then bent his face to hers. He could feel no breath coming from between her lips. With horror, he realized that she was dead.

Dead? How could she possibly be dead?

He looked from her pale face to the destroyed art case and realized that the blast must have done something more to her than just knocking her down. He remembered the noble he had nearly toppled. The Augmented nobles could not survive a fall. And if the fall had killed Marie-Ange that meant . . . Marie-Ange was Augmented.

John shuddered and drew back from her, laying her body down gently on the floor. He stared at her lovely, pure white face, its enamel coating cracked, and saw a cyborg instead of the natural beauty he loved.

John scrabbled to his feet and lurched away, his legs feeling like rubber, ears ringing. His art case lay shattered next to the remains of his love. He didn't look back as he stumbled down the dim corridor, not knowing or caring where he was going.

ℬ Φ ℭ

The lights were still not functioning in Adelaide's laboratory

Perhaps I should go and see if I can assist the Palace Engineer and his staff to get them back on. I can't work without light.

She picked her way back to the table where her Automated Dauphin lay. She studied the immobile face and caressed his cold, metal cheek before lifting the cover over him.

A loud bang shook the room, rattling loose equipment, and Adelaide fell against the prone automaton. She gasped. Her heart pounding, she pushed herself back up.

Another bomb?

She surveyed the laboratory for damage but in the dim

light, it was hard to see. Adelaide heard a man's voice shouting out in the corridor outside her laboratory door. He sounded panicked. She picked her way across the expansive room to the door, swearing to herself as she dodged equipment piled up on the floor. Reaching the door, she slipped out into the dark hallway. Sunlight streamed in from the tall windows at one end of the hallway. Adelaide squinted. She could see a pile of clothing lying in the middle of the hallway and some sort of wooden case, its contents spilled all over the marble floor. Had someone panicked, trying to leave but dropped their possessions? Adelaide shook her head. Sometimes the occupants of Versailles could be so irrational. She drew closer and realized that the pile of clothing was a woman, collapsed on the ground. Adelaide hurried to her side and gasped when she recognized the crumpled figure.

"Marie-Ange! Are you hurt?" She dropped to her knees beside the young girl's head. She couldn't spot any visible blood or injury.

Oh no. It must be her heart.

She placed a hand on the girl's throat and could feel no thrumming as blood moved through her artery. Adelaide leaned close to Marie-Ange's face. She wasn't breathing but her skin was still warm.

"Oh, no, no, my dear girl," she gasped. She smoothed Marie-Ange's hair back and let her hand rest there. Too late. She was too late. If only she had come upon Marie-Ange a few minutes later, she might have been able to restart her heart with the modulator.

Unless.

Unless she could use an electric charge to restart the clockwork mechanism. Perhaps she wasn't too late. Quickly, she had to move quickly. If the girl's heart had only just stopped, there were precious few minutes before her brain was damaged beyond repair. She grabbed the girl's shoulders, trying to lift her but realized that even though Marie-Ange was a petite girl, she was still too heavy for Adelaide to carry. The hallway was deserted; no burly ushers there to help lift the girl.

Probably just as well. I don't want anyone seeing what I'm going to attempt. It's probably illegal or immoral.

Adelaide stood and, taking fistfuls of the girl's elaborate Court gown, started dragging her along the floor. The marble floor was slick enough that she was able to move Marie-Ange and soon reached the doorway to her laboratory. She opened the door, checked both ways to make sure she was unobserved, and dragged the girl inside.

She was fairly certain that attempting to raise the dead would be frowned upon but she wasn't going to give up on Marie-Ange. Not yet.

Adelaide hoisted the young noblewoman's limp body onto a work table and, with a knife, tore open the heavy embroidered bodice encasing Marie-Ange's chest. Cursing at the need for multiple layers of constricting clothing the Court ladies insisted on, she cut and tugged until she had bared Marie-Ange's chest. Working quickly, she placed electrodes on the girl's delicate skin and cranked the little battery that she had constructed for use with the Automated Dauphin. She had no idea how much energy would be required to restart Marie-Ange's mechanical heart. Too much would destroy it. Not enough would do nothing and Marie-Ange would die. If she wasn't already dead.

Breathing deeply, Adelaide allowed a small amount of charge to flow into the electrodes. Marie-Ange's body jolted. Adelaide turned off the power and bent her head to listen for the rushing of blood moving through her mechanical heart. Nothing. Her palms were sweating so she wiped them on her work apron. More energy was needed. She cranked the battery again and let the charge flow, more this time. The girl's torso lifted from the table but her body fell back, unmoving.

"Marie-Ange! Can you hear me, *chérie*?" Adelaide cried. The girl lay still on the table. There was no response. She was gone. Adelaide gripped her fist and slammed it against the table.

"No! No, this cannot be. You can't be dead, dear child, you can't be dead!" Her tears fell, unwanted, hot against her cheeks. She wiped them away with a rough hand. She stared down at the dead girl in front of her. Her chest was scarred from the surgery to give her a clockwork heart. There were new burn marks, some from the electrodes but looking closer, Adelaide could see that the skin over her heart was red and swollen. Something brutal had happened to her and damaged her heart.

What happened out there in the hallway? The box! What was in that box next to Marie-Ange? I need to find out.

Adelaide dashed to the door of the darkened room, banging her knee again in her haste. When would they get the electricity working again? She turned back and grabbed one of her portable electric lights.

ℰ Φ ℭ

John staggered through the endless rooms and hallways of Versailles in a stupor, his ears still ringing from the blast. He couldn't find his way out of this elegant maze. Courtiers and servants walked briskly by in the dim hallways, paying no attention to him. Marie-Ange was dead. The thought droned on in his mind.

My love is dead. But . . . she was a cyborg. Augmented. Not a natural beauty after all. How could I have—

With a start, he realized that he was back in the same chequered marble hallway where he had left Marie-Ange's body. Trembling, he saw his wrecked art case, brushes and paints scattered across the marble floor. Its wooden lid was partially smashed and the latch was twisted. The art case was laying there, broken, but his broken love was gone.

Had someone already discovered her corpse, here in the dimly lit hallway? Or perhaps she had not truly been dead? Perhaps her mechanical body was not as susceptible to the Underground's stun device as they had thought. He shuddered, picturing a mechanical Marie-Ange, unkillable and inhuman.

No, that is too horrible. Someone must have taken her body away but left the case, thinking it unimportant.

He drew nearer the case with the incriminating device, the weapon that had delivered Marie-Ange a killing blow.

John realized that he needed to gather the box and the materials and get out of the Palace if he hoped to escape with his life. He hadn't been thinking clearly. The remains of the stun device alone were enough to get him imprisoned and executed. He crouched down and started scooping the detritus of his career back into the box, slowly at first but then faster as he realized that he probably didn't have much time before someone discovered him. His head pounded with pain. Lights exploded behind his eyelids when he blinked. John lurched to his feet, gripping the case against his chest. Trying to hold it closed, its sharp edges digging into his body. He barely registered the pain. He glanced around, trying to get his bearings.

I'll head towards a window and try to figure out where I am.

He staggered away down the hallway, turning towards the daylight. Behind him, he heard a door click open. He quickened his step, trying to move quietly. His heart was pounding as he turned a corner. He finally recognized where he was and hurried to the servants' hall, heading for the tradesmen's entrance. John hoped Jeanne wouldn't be there. He didn't want to encounter her smiling face and know it was the last time. His time as a Court Painter was over. His dream was dead. Marie-Ange was dead. He knew he'd never return to the Palace of Versailles.

ᘐ Φ ᘓ

Adelaide switched on her little electric lantern as she stepped into the hallway. She thought she heard footsteps and strained to hear, but they disappeared into the distance. She walked down the dim hallway, shining her light. When she got to where she had discovered Marie-Ange, she saw that the floor was bare. The box was gone.

"Damnation," she swore softly. No box. That meant that the mysterious assailant must have come back for it while Adelaide was trying to resuscitate Marie-Ange.

He—it had to have been a man—had left Marie-Ange just lying there on the floor. Did he go to get assistance? Or had he thought she was dead? Was he responsible for her heart stopping?

Adelaide needed to find out what was in that box. She paced around the hallway, holding her light high for better visibility. Perhaps he had dropped something, left a clue.

She suddenly spied the wooden handle of something behind a pedestal. She stepped closer and reached down. It was a paint brush, the bristles near the bottom encrusted with blue paint. So perhaps the mysterious wooden box had been an artist's case? Was the assailant a painter? Adelaide groaned. So many of the Court ladies commissioned paintings, it was hard to keep track of the painters coming and going at the Palace.

Adelaide turned and went back to her laboratory. She stopped short when she saw Marie-Ange's body. She had been too young to die. A surge of anger filled Adelaide.

"I will find out who did this to you, ma chère. Your murderer will be punished," she promised.

Twelve

It was dark when John finally stumbled in the door of his house, clutching his broken art case as if it were a lifeline. His trip home from Versailles had passed in a blur. He was shivering uncontrollably from the coldness inside him. Stiffly, like an old man, he placed the wooden box on a side table. His hands were shaking. He stared at them.

Is this what a killer's hands look like?

What have I done?

Images of Marie-Ange sprawled on the marble floor filled his mind. Her beautiful face, so still in death. He had killed her. His Marie-Ange. She was leaving the Court to be with him and he had killed her. He tried to calm the trembling but his breath came in gasps and he needed to sit down. He jerked into motion, heading for his sitting room.

He heard a knock on the front door and started. Had they discovered his crime already? A whimper escaped his lips. He crept to the side window, peering out at the street. Henri and Arthur waited there, looking up and down the street. John let out a quick breath of relief. He opened the front door, saying,

"Come in, quickly."

Once inside, Henri scrutinized John's face and said, "You look awful. What happened at the Palace?" John shook his head, unable to trust himself to speak, and beckoned them into his sitting room, lighting a single lamp. He poured bourbon for all of them and sucked down a glass before speaking.

"The device. It went off. It went off . . ." He trailed off, unable to continue, breathing hard. Arthur sat forward, his drink untouched.

"Did it work? Is the Queen dead?" he asked. John dropped his gaze and pinched the bridge of his nose, struggling for control.

"It worked, Arthur. The device worked. But it did not kill the Queen. It killed . . . it killed Marie-Ange."

Henri groaned, dropping his head into his hands.

"Marie-Ange? Who is Marie-Ange?" asked Arthur. Henri raised his head, his face drawn and solemn.

"Marie-Ange was the young noblewoman John was in love with," he murmured. John's face grew even paler and he nodded.

"But I do not understand. How did the device kill her? It was meant to disrupt the automatons. Did it malfunction?" asked Arthur. Henri and Arthur stared at John, waiting for a response. After a long silence, John said,

"She must have been Augmented in some vital way. Perhaps she had, I don't know, a mechanical heart? I had no idea. I didn't know she was Augmented and now she is dead. I killed her. I killed her," he moaned, covering his face to hide his tears.

"I am so sorry, John. We never meant for anything like

that to happen. But how did you not know that she was Augmented? Surely she would have mentioned it?" said Henri.

"No. We had so little time together. Stolen moments. Ah, Henri, she was so very beautiful. I thought she was the ideal beauty." His voice broke, choked with tears. "I wanted to paint her. She would have been my muse. No-one would have been able to deny my talent, not with images of her beauty filling my canvases."

"John," Henri said gently, "No-one can deny your talent. Your talent is in you, not the models you paint. You can still be a great painter, even without your Marie-Ange." Henri's eyes were full of compassion. John's face sagged at the thought of never painting Marie-Ange. Of never again tasting her lips. He drew a shuddering breath.

"Without Marie-Ange. But I can never return to the Court. How will I find subjects to paint?" As he spoke, he remembered sketching the plump woman in the gardens. It had felt so easy, so natural to sketch her face, despite its lack of beauty.

"I am afraid it is not just the Court that is barred to you," Arthur interjected. "With the Queen still alive, it is too dangerous for you to remain in France. It is only a matter of time before someone discovers your part in Marie-Ange's death. You and Henri must leave France immediately."

Henri nodded, and leaned forward, clasping John's shoulder.

"I knew this was a possibility. The carriage will be here to take me to Calais soon. You must come with me. I'll help you pack, mon frère."

They ascended the stairs to John's bedroom in silence. John pulled down his valise and began packing his clothes in a daze. He picked up an enameled brooch from the top of the dresser. It was a delicate painting of a primrose that had reminded him of Marie-Ange. *I can't live without you.* The meaning mocked him now. He had intended to give it to her, a secret message of love, but it was too late. He placed it back down. He had no need for it now. Marie-Ange had no need for it now. He stifled a sob.

They moved to John's studio and he scanned the walls, seeing the few paintings that had not sold. They were of pretty strangers, devoid of life and feeling. How could he have thought they were interesting? How many of them were Augmented, mockeries of the beauty he had longed to portray?

"I don't need to keep any of these," he told Henri. "Just pack up the paints and brushes. You'll have to use my old art case." Henri raised his eyebrows but didn't comment.

The steam carriage arrived just as they were bringing down the valise and boxes. Isabelle sat inside, peeking out the window into the darkness. She exchanged kisses with Henri.

"You're not leaving France without me," she murmured. He grinned and squeezed her. There was a flurry of farewells, then Arthur was waving to them from John's doorway as the steam carriage hissed away. They passed brightly lit cafes, full of people. John watched them, finding intriguing faces but none of them were Marie-Ange.

Would the people in England be as interesting? There was no Augmentation there, none of the artifice of France.

He caught Henri's eye. His brother sat with his arm wrapped around Isabelle's shoulders. He looked happy, relaxed. John wondered at that. How could Henri be so accepting of his impending exile?

"We are having a grand adventure, *non*?" Henri said, beaming. He clapped John's shoulder. "We're heading to a new life. We will create great art in England and when the monarchy changes, we can return to France."

John gazed back out at the passing scenery, the familiar sights of Montmartre. He didn't know if he'd ever see them again. He wasn't sure he cared. His voice was low and quiet as he responded.

"Yes, mon frère."

Thirteen

London, 1881

The rain streamed down the window of the quiet, cozy tea-room. John sat watching it, uncomfortable in his damp trousers. He was forever being caught in a shower here in London. He never knew when to expect rain. The hot steaming tea warmed him but did nothing to dry his clothing. He sipped the tea slowly, enjoying the tannic taste, and considered ordering cream scones. He had to be more careful with his money now. His clientele were not all rich aristocrats these days.

With that thought, an image of Marie-Ange rose in his mind. He swallowed the lump in his throat, willing himself not to break down again. His lovely muse, struck down by his own hand. He knew he would always feel guilty for that. If only he had known about her Augmentation. He could have warned her somehow. He took another sip of tea, its heat calming him, washing away the salt of his suppressed tears.

He gestured to the waitress to order, needing some food to settle his nerves. Appearing after a glacially slow wait, the waitress dropped the plate onto the table without a smile. These Londoners weren't the friendliest of people. John devoured the scones, and his mind turned to his brother.

It's too bad Henri isn't here. He would love these scones. They don't have that off flavor that French pastries have.

Henri and Isabelle were off in the wilds of Scotland on their honeymoon. Henri had wanted to try his hand at painting Scottish landscapes, misty in the rain. John smiled as he thought of them, so happy on their wedding day. Despite his fervor for Marie-Ange and his fantasies of their future together, John could never imagine actually marrying her. She had been too much an ideal, not truly a person in his eyes. And yet, her lovely face still haunted his dreams.

The door to the tearoom opened in a burst of raindrops and wind. A hunched old woman bundled up in ragged clothing stood in the doorway. She walked in, dripping water all over the floor and plopped herself into a chair. She had rags wrapped around her grubby hands, but her red, chilblained fingers were exposed to the cold. The waitress approached her, mouth turned down in a sneer.

"You get out of 'ere, Mary. I don't have room for the likes of you," she told the old woman.

"Nah, don't throw me out, ducks, I 'ave some money for a nice hot cuppa," the old woman said, showing her coins. The waitress tsked but took the coins and went to fetch the woman's tea. John caught the old woman's eye and smiled.

"It is a nasty day to be out and about," he said. She nodded in return and unwound some of the rags from around her neck and head. Her frizzy grey hair was topped by a surprisingly dashing little hat. John almost laughed aloud at the absurdity but a thought occurred to him.

"My dear woman, may I sketch you?" he asked her. Her eyes went round in surprise.

"'Oo, me? You want to make a picture of me? You must be maggoty!" She cackled and took the proffered cup from the waitress, who still didn't smile. With a murmur of pleasure, the old woman slurped her tea. John pulled out his sketchpad and pencil.

"Do you mind?" he asked again. She waved a hand at him.

"Go on then."

John settled down to sketch the weathered old woman, hoping to capture the life embedded in those lines and wrinkles. She was no Marie-Ange, but John could see the beauty in her rough, aged visage.

Henri, *mon frère, tu avais raison.*

A smile touched John's mouth as he drew.

FINIS

About the author

BJ Sikes is a 5'6" ape descendant who is inordinately fond of a good strong cup of tea, Doc Marten boots, and fancy dress. She lives with two large cats, two small children and one editor-author.

Acknowledgements

This book would not exist without AJ Sikes and his amazing editorial skills and brainstorming sessions. I would have come unglued without Dover Whitecliff's unceasing support and encouragement as well as the writing advice and beta reading. Thank you both from the bottom of my clockwork heart.

I also want to thank Alex Barszap for his patience with my obtuse questions and for his advice about clockwork, robots, and other mechanical mysteries. Anything I got right about these cyborgs is solely due to him and if I got anything wrong, it's not Alex's fault.

Thank you Margaret and Charlotte for your inspiration, motivation, and great hugs.

My deepest thanks to Emperor Shen Nung for discovering tea in 2,737 B.C.

Printed in Great Britain
by Amazon